"You wouldn't be the mystery lady by any chance, would you?"

At Eve's blank look Gabriel added, "That's what my secretary's been calling you ever since you made the appointment." He leaned back in his chair and studied her. "So, Ms Mystery Lady, are you going to tell me your name?"

"Before I do, I must insist that you don't reveal my identity to anyone."

"Certainly. I'd do that whether or not I decide to take you on as a client."

"*You* decide?"

"I've been known to turn down a case or two. Let's just say I'm choosy."

From the looks of the private eye's office, Eve wondered how he could afford to be choosy. Her courage wavered. Then she reminded herself he was her last resort. "I'll make it well worth your while, Mr. Bouvier." She straightened in her chair and crossed her legs.

She had great legs, Gabriel noticed. "Okay, so what's your problem?"

"It's a man...."

JoAnn Ross says she has something in common with the heroine of *Eve's Choice*, her fourteenth Temptation. "Like Eve, I used to be a workaholic. Then one day I realized that life was passing me by, and I'd better learn to relax and enjoy it." JoAnn still works hard, but she takes some time out from her busy writing career to enjoy her phenomenal success, baseball—she's a die-hard New York Yankees fan—and life with her husband in Phoenix, Arizona.

Books by JoAnn Ross

HARLEQUIN TEMPTATION

HARLEQUIN INTRIGUE

Eve's Choice

JoANN ROSS

Harlequin Books

TORONTO • NEW YORK • LONDON
AMSTERDAM • PARIS • SYDNEY • HAMBURG
STOCKHOLM • ATHENS • TOKYO • MILAN

To Jay, the lagniappe of my life

Published October 1988

ISBN 0-373-25321-4

1

GABRIEL BOUVIER WAS HOT.

It was July, the temperature was in the nineties and the level of humidity was inching toward a record high, even for New Orleans. The French doors to his cramped second-story office were open, but the air outside was torrid and heavy, providing no relief as he watched a baseball game on the portable television that was perched on the corner of his cluttered antique desk.

It was the bottom of the seventh, and the Mets' Jesse Orosco was on his way to shutting out the Braves at home. Gabriel figured he knew exactly how frustrated the Braves were feeling. His shirt was sticking to his back, and he was fantasizing about closing up shop for the day and going out for a tall, cold beer when she walked in the door, looking fresh and cool in a sleeveless white silk dress, sheer white stockings, high-heeled white pumps and a wide-brimmed white straw hat with a navy-and-white-striped band. Beneath the hat her hair was coiled into a neat bun at the back of her neck.

Turning off the television, he took swift, judicious inventory, as much from force of habit as personal interest. Once a cop, always a cop. Age between twenty-eight and thirty-one and height five feet, five-and-one half inches, weight 115 pounds, hair blond, color of eyes indiscernible due to a pair of white-framed, oversize sunglasses. The scent of bath soap emanated from honey-hued skin that bore no distinguishing scars or birthmarks—at least, none that he could see.

"There wasn't anyone in the waiting room," she said to explain entering his office without being announced.

"Sorry about that; my secretary, Fayrene, was called out of town this morning. Her sister just had a baby girl. Nine pounds, twelve and a half ounces."

"That's quite a large baby."

"Sure is," Gabriel said agreeably. He gestured toward a chair on the visitors' side of the desk. "Why don't you have a seat? Your name wouldn't be Wonderly by any chance, would it?"

"No." She perched on the very edge of the chair, clutching her white calfskin purse as if she were afraid Gabriel might suddenly jump up, leap across the desk and snatch it away. Her fingernails were buffed to a glossy sheen, her knuckles white.

"You remind me a lot of her," he continued conversationally. "Although her hair was red and yours is blond. But the situation is much the same; a beautiful, secretive woman shows up in the office of a ruggedly handsome private detective. Of course you're obviously not going to turn out to have killed my partner because I work alone, but the opening scene is pretty much the same, wouldn't you say?"

She glanced back nervously toward the door, as if contemplating escape. "I haven't the faintest idea what you're talking about."

"You haven't read *The Maltese Falcon*?"

"No."

"You should. It's a classic."

"I'll keep that in mind."

"You do that." There was a moment of silence. "You are the mystery lady, aren't you?" he asked finally.

"Mystery lady?"

"That's what my secretary's been calling you ever since you made the appointment yesterday. Fayrene's read *The Maltese Falcon*."

"I think I saw the movie once. On the late show."

Gabriel nodded approvingly. "Great flick. Bogie played Spade just the way Hammett wrote him."

He leaned back in his chair, put his elbows on its scarred wooden arms and studied her over linked fingers. Overhead a lazy paddle fan beat ineffectively at the soupy air, reminding Gabriel that he'd hoped to get out of the office early.

"So, Ms Mystery Lady, are you going to tell me your name, or are we going to play twenty questions all afternoon?"

"Before I do, I must insist that you not reveal my identity to anyone," she said after another lengthy pause.

"Certainly. I'd do that whether or not I decide to take you on as a client."

"You decide?"

"I've been known to turn down a case or two. Some of my colleagues have accused me of being unreasonably picky, but hey, that's what makes horse races, right?"

"Excuse me?"

He decided to try again. "My Granddaddy Bouvier used to say that if all of us liked the same thing, every man in the country would be after Grandma."

Her only response was a long, slightly confused stare.

"Let's just say I'm choosy," he said.

From the looks of Gabriel Bouvier's office, Eve Whitfield wondered how the man could afford to be choosy about his terms of employment. The badly scuffed black and white tiles covering the floor appeared to be original, rather than a failed attempt to recreate a trendy, art deco atmosphere. The walls, painted in a faded institutional gray, were lined with metal file cabinets and bookshelves, the tops of which, like the ancient desk, were piled high with dog-eared manila folders, lined yellow pads, newspapers, law books and telephone directories from what appeared to be every parish in the state.

For what had to be the millionth time since she'd made the decision to hire a private investigator, Eve felt her courage waning. Then, reminding herself that she had exhausted all other avenues and this man was her last resort, she stiffened her spine, as well as her wavering resolve.

"I'm capable of making it well worth your while, Mr. Bouvier." Her voice had the unmistakable ring of expensive finishing schools. Oddly, Gabriel found himself more intrigued than annoyed by her condescending attitude. He also wished she'd take off the damn glasses.

"I'm afraid that's not the way it works," he explained patiently. "You see, we begin with you telling me your name. Your real name. Which is only fair since you already know mine. Then you tell me exactly what trouble you're in, without holding anything back because you're afraid it might prove embarrassing." He gave her an encouraging grin. "Believe me, you couldn't tell me anything I haven't already heard."

"I've not a single doubt of that," she murmured.

Gabriel decided not to take offense. At least not yet. "Finally," he continued amiably, "if the case interests me, I take it on."

"And if it doesn't interest you?"

"Then we shake hands, you return to the secure, gilded confines of Audubon Place and I go back to watching the Braves lose another one."

"I don't live at Audubon Place."

Damn. It wasn't like him to read someone wrong. His livelihood, and every once in a while his life, depended on accurate first impressions. Audubon Place was the ritziest and most exclusive street in New Orleans. The neighborhood was walled, and the street blocked by an enormous gate, permitting the residents to be extremely selective about whom they allowed within it. If this wasn't the quintessential Uptown Girl, he'd eat his private investigator's license.

"So if you don't reside in one of those regal mansions in the silk-stocking district, where do you live, Ms—"

"Whitfield," she filled in reluctantly. "Eve Whitfield."

Gabriel whistled under his breath. Talk about your heavy hitters. "As in Whitfield Towers."

It was not a question, but Eve answered, anyway. "That's right."

"And Whitfield Palace Hotels. 'When deluxe will no longer do,'" he quoted the world-famous slogan.

"My father didn't believe in doing anything in a halfhearted manner."

"So I've heard."

It was beginning to come to him. Douglas Whitfield had been stricken with a fatal heart attack while playing a game of tennis on the family court one balmy Sunday afternoon two years ago this past spring. He'd been playing with his daughter, Gabriel recalled belatedly.

"His death must have been quite a loss," he said.

"It was. Although fortunately I didn't have time to dwell on it. There was, after all, Whitfield Palace Hotels to tend to."

"I can imagine that a multinational empire needs a great deal of hands-on supervision," Gabriel said dryly.

Eve lifted her chin. "My father would not have wanted me to waste precious time grieving. Business was his life blood, Mr. Bouvier. He was an extremely successful, hard-driving man. He expected nothing less from his employees."

"How about from his daughter?"

"Especially from his daughter." Her tone was an unmistakable warning; Gabriel could practically see the No Trespassing signs going up all around her chair.

Deciding that there was no point in driving away a wealthy client by insulting her relationship with her deceased father, he returned the conversation to its original track. "So, Ms Eve Whitfield, what's your problem?"

Her mouth had gone suddenly dry. Eve swallowed visibly. "It's a man."

"It usually is," he said agreeably, pouring her a glass of water from a pitcher on the credenza behind him.

"Thank you." She sipped the tepid water as she tried to arrange her thoughts. "You don't understand. I'm not involved with this man."

"Oh, no?"

"No. I merely want you to locate him for me."

Gabriel was hot, sticky and tired of dragging the story out of Ms Uptown Eve Whitfield bit by agonizing bit. "If you're not involved with him, why do you want me to track him down?"

Stalling to shore up her suddenly crumbling nerve, Eve took a long drink. "Because Harry Keegan used to own some land upriver where Whitfield Hotels intends to build a new New Orleans Whitfield Palace," she said finally, relying on the story she'd come up with over several cups of hot black coffee this morning. "You see, he sold the land to our real-estate department, but left town before our legal department could get his signature on a quitclaim deed."

As she handed Gabriel her empty glass, he couldn't help noticing that her hands were shaking. Not much. But just enough to show that beneath that cool finishing-school exterior the woman was a bundle of raw nerves.

"Obviously we can't begin construction until we've cleared up the matter of ownership rights," she continued a bit breathlessly, as if anxious to get the story over with. "After all, it wouldn't do for Whitfield Palace Hotels to be sued for real-estate fraud."

"Daddy would probably roll over in his tomb," Gabriel drawled.

She looked inclined to comment on his flippant statement but apparently decided against it. "So you see, Mr. Bouvier, that's where you come in. You find Harry Keegan, he signs the deed and receives his final check, Whitfield Palace Hotels can begin construction and you earn a generous fee." She flashed him a smile, the first he'd witnessed. It was quick, bright and entirely feigned. "Everyone comes out ahead."

Gabriel refrained from answering immediately. Instead, he locked his hands behind his head. The muscles in his upper arms swelled against his shirtsleeves as he swiveled in his chair, studying Eve Whitfield with a slow, silent interest.

His expression remained neutral, but as he continued his scrutiny, Eve was uncomfortably aware of the sharp intelligence lurking in those fathomless dark eyes. Although she was a successful, independent woman, she suddenly felt like a schoolgirl summoned to the principal's office. It was all she could do not to squirm under the man's unwavering glance.

Small beads of sweat formed on her upper lip; she resisted the urge to wipe them away. The ceiling fan continued its futile battle with the moist air, the low hum of its electric motor punctuated every few seconds by a rusty squeak. Time slowed to a snail's pace as they studied each other over the cluttered surface of the mahogany desk. Gabriel's expression was openly skeptical; hers remained coolly serene.

She was good, Gabriel acknowledged. Damn good. She was also a liar.

"Sorry," he finally said, after what had seemed an eternity to Eve, "but I don't think I'm the man for the job."

For a fleeting moment Eve's anxiety bubbled to the surface, allowing the color to drain away beneath her golden tan. She forced her whirling mind to concentrate on the fact that she was a Whitfield. Whitfields never took no for an answer. It was the first of many valuable lessons her father had taught her.

"I beg your pardon?"

Gabriel nodded approvingly. "Very well done," he said. "Cool disdain, with just a touch of arrogance. Your elocution teacher was obviously worth every penny."

Eve rose abruptly. "I don't enjoy being insulted, Mr. Bouvier."

Gabriel found her sudden flare of anger intriguing. It demonstrated that there were hidden fires simmering under all those layers of ice after all. He wondered if Eve Whitfield knew that she'd just handed him a valuable insight into her personality; from the slight wash of color staining her cheeks, he decided that she not only realized that fact, but was regretting it, as well.

"And I don't enjoy being lied to, Ms Whitfield."

Touché. Experiencing a sense of impending defeat, Eve rubbed her temples wearily with her fingertips. No rings, Gabriel noticed. Nor bracelets. Her only jewelry consisted of a slim, gold-banded watch with Roman numerals and a pair of perfectly matched pearls adorning her earlobes. He wondered if the pearls had been a gift from her father. Or perhaps a lover.

"I didn't lie to you," she said at length.

Gabriel's only response was an arched brow.

Eve was momentarily shaken by the way the man suddenly reminded her of her father. But that was ridiculous. Douglas Whitfield had been an extraordinary man; there had been no limits to his achievements. If this cramped, stultifying office located above a Royal Street antique shop was any indication, Gabriel Bouvier was a classic example of a lifelong underachiever. Still, she couldn't deny that his prolonged silence was strangely intimidating.

"All right. Perhaps I wasn't altogether truthful," she admitted haltingly. "But you have to understand that this is extremely difficult for me." She paused, giving him a chance to break in. To reassure her. To beg for another opportunity to take her case.

Nothing. Gabriel merely sat there, well-muscled arms now folded over his chest, observing her with the same patience a well-fed cat might employ when playing with a mouse.

Eve took a deep breath and began again. "I was assured that you were the best man for the job." This was a better tack. She'd never met a man impervious to flattery. "And believe me, Mr. Bouvier, Whitfield Palace Hotels is accustomed to dealing only with the best."

Silence. Moisture had begun to gather in the cleft between her breasts. "With the fee you'd earn from this simple case, you could buy air-conditioning for your office," she offered encouragingly. "Or even move upriver to the CBD."

Although Eve could not honestly envision Gabriel Bouvier among the concrete canyons formed by the glass-and-steel high-rise buildings, she couldn't imagine anyone turning down an opportunity to work in the bustling, high-energy atmosphere of the Central Business District. Whitfield Towers had long been a Canal Street landmark.

"I like it here," Gabriel said simply. "And if I had air-conditioning, I'd have to close the French doors. Then I wouldn't be able to smell that bougainvillea on the balcony railing." He smiled. "Although I'll admit I'm not much of an expert when it comes to identifying the wealth of foliage that thrives in our tropical climate, I'd really miss that bougainvillea."

Eve was nonplussed. "Oh."

"Why don't you sit down," he suggested pleasantly, "and begin your story again. This time omitting the fiction."

Once again Eve was struck by the way he managed to convey such authority with a mere glance. A quiet tone. Beginning to realize that she was dealing with a more complex man than he appeared at first glance, she followed his suggestion.

"I really am looking for Harry Keegan," she said, tugging her pristine white skirt over her knees as she crossed her legs.

"But not for anything dealing with quitclaim deeds."

"No. I'm afraid that was an elaboration."

"It was a lie, Ms Whitfield," Gabriel corrected calmly. "And if I agree to work for you, the first thing that you need to understand is that I insist my clients be honest with me."

"I understand."

Gabriel smiled his satisfaction with having gotten that little matter clarified. "Why are you looking for Keegan?"

"It's a long story."

"I'm not going anywhere."

Eve studied him thoughtfully for a long, drawn-out moment. His face was chiseled and full of character. Lines fanned out from deep-set eyes the color of aged bourbon; his nose appeared to have been broken on more than one occasion, and a thin white scar cut across his square jaw. It was the face of a man used to living life on his own terms, even if those terms at times included violence and danger. It was also, she decided finally, the face of a man she could trust.

"Harry Keegan is a friend of my mother's."

"How close a friend?"

"*She* thinks they're getting married."

"What does Keegan think? Or do you know?"

"No one knows what the man is up to," Eve admitted. "Because he's disappeared."

"So you want me to find him for your mother."

"Yes. No. Well, in a way, but—"

"Which is it? Yes? Or no?"

"Harry broke off a dinner engagement with my mother last week, claiming some sort of family emergency."

"Perhaps that's exactly what it was."

"Perhaps. But Dixie believes otherwise. Although it's not the first time he's left the city—he says his work as a free-lance business consultant involves a great deal of travel—it is the first time he hasn't called her during his absence."

"So since she hasn't heard from the guy, your mother's convinced that something has happened to him."

"Exactly."

"There's always the chance that Keegan decided things were getting too serious and simply moved on."

"That is, of course, one possibility," Eve conceded, looking very closely at a framed George Rodrigue print depicting Cajun life. Gabriel sensed that she was uncomfortable talking about personal things.

"One your mother refuses to accept," he said quietly, helping her out.

She was no longer studying the print; now she was looking straight at him. "Richard Owens suggested that you were more perceptive than you appear at first glance."

"Yeah, I pay him to say that to prospective clients."

She did not smile. "I hate seeing my mother upset."

"Most of us do," he agreed amiably.

"In an attempt to soothe Dixie's anxiety, I promised to hire a private detective to locate Keegan."

"And return him, safe and sound, to his beloved's side."

She shook her head. "Not exactly. I do want you to find Harry. But then I want you to make certain that he promises to stay away from my mother."

"If you're looking for a goon to break the guy's legs, I'm afraid you've come to the wrong man, Ms Whitfield."

She gasped at his misunderstanding. "That's not what I'm asking at all," she professed earnestly. "I merely want you to offer him an incentive."

"By incentive, you mean money."

There was no point in denying it. "Yes."

"Why are you so determined to buy the guy off?"

Thoughts of Dixie and Harry Keegan overrode her strangely frazzled nerves, and Eve sighed, depressed by the idea of her sweet, innocent mother succumbing to such a skilled con man. Hadn't she promised her father, in those last precious moments of his life, that she'd watch out for his delightfully scatterbrained wife?

Unfortunately keeping an eye on Dixie Whitfield's activities was proving to be a full-time job. She often wondered how her father had managed to accomplish anything, let alone build a worldwide empire. *Oh, Daddy,* she apologized mentally, *I'm trying not to let you down.*

Gabriel watched the small dark cloud move across her face and wondered at its cause. "Ms Whitfield?"

Eve shook her head, forcing her thoughts back to the present. "Harry Keegan arrived in New Orleans three months ago, claiming to be a retired businessman. Despite several attempts on my part to learn the exact nature of his business, the man remained steadfastly vague. Naturally, I became suspicious."

"Naturally."

She glanced at him sharply, seeking evidence of amusement. When his expression remained inscrutable, she continued. "Since Keegan refused to cooperate with me, I had no choice but to have him investigated."

"I'm sure your father would have approved of your initiative."

Once again she searched for humor at her expense. Once again she failed to find any. "It's precisely what he would have done. Under the circumstances."

"Of course. So what did your investigation uncover?"

Reaching into her bag, she pulled out a thick sheaf of papers, which she handed to him. "As you can see, Harry Keegan is no more a retired businessman than I am Mardi Gras Queen."

Gabriel glanced up from the pages he was perusing. "You could be, you know."

"Could be what?"

"Queen of the Mardi Gras. Of course you'd have to loosen up a little, learn how to enjoy life, instead of hiding away in the executive offices of Whitfield Towers, but you're certainly good-looking enough."

Eve frowned. "I prefer to be judged on my intelligence, rather than my appearance, Mr. Bouvier."

He ran a finger down the side of his nose as he slowly, intimately perused her exquisitely shaped face, her slender nose, her soft, feminine mouth, ending at her stubborn chin. He wished, not for the first time, that she'd take off the sunglasses.

"In order for a man to do that, Ms Whitfield," he drawled sapiently, "you'd have to take to wearing a paper bag over your head."

She shot him a stern look. "When Mr. Owens was citing your expertise, he failed to mention that you were a chauvinist."

"Just calling them as I see them. So Owens and Martin were the ones who recommended me?"

Eve was vastly relieved to have the conversation return to her reason for coming here today. "That's right. Their firm does a great deal of security work for Whitfield Palace Hotels. They were the ones who compiled that report on Harry Keegan."

Along with the papers was a newspaper clipping, obviously a society page item. The photo showed an attractive woman in her fifties standing beside a man who, if Gabriel hadn't been holding concrete proof of the man's criminal bent, he would have immediately taken for a cop. Harry Keegan looked like a cop: broad shoulders, barrel chest, close-cropped iron-gray hair, lantern jaw.

He was wearing an ill-fitting white dinner jacket that looked like a rental. He also looked uncomfortable as hell having his picture taken, which, given his record, was understandable, Gabriel considered. There were probably outstanding warrants in police stations all over the country for the man.

Gabriel put the papers down on his desk. "I will admit that the guy has an impressive criminal record."

"I'd hardly call his activities impressive," she corrected briskly. "Harry Keegan has spent nearly half of his sixty-two years in prison."

"At least you can't accuse him of being an underachiever," Gabriel pointed out. "Why didn't you ask Owens and Martin to find him? Since they'd already begun the investigation."

"Mr. Owens explained to me that his firm, while certainly up to the task, preferred to remain an information-gathering service."

Gabriel was well acquainted with the Owens and Martin Agency. Definitely not bourbon-bottle-in-the-desk-drawer detectives like Sam Spade or Philip Marlowe, they had the manpower and expertise to deal with cases ranging from routine surveillance to million-dollar industrial espionage.

"Meaning they don't want to get their hands dirty with common, ordinary fieldwork. Especially when there are guys like me willing to muck around in the mud."

"I'm sure that's not what Mr. Owens meant at all," she protested.

"Of course it was," he said without rancor. "I'll want to speak to your mother. As soon as possible."

"You're not going to tell her—"

"That her daughter is planning to buy off her lover?" Gabriel broke in. "No. I figure you've got her best interests at heart. Besides, there's always the chance that Keegan will turn the offer down."

"And pigs will fly," Eve muttered. "First you have to find him."

"That's precisely what I intend to do."

"Does that mean you're taking the case?"

"I suppose it does."

Eve's relief was palpable as she pulled a checkbook from her bag. "I'll pay you five hundred dollars a day, plus expenses," she said, beginning to fill out a check. "Will ten days' advance be satisfactory?"

This was definitely turning out to be an amazing day. The way it was going, Gabriel half expected Mary Astor to waltz in the door, surrounded by a cloud of Chanel No 5, and get him involved with the fat man in a search for a fabled black bird. As he watched the slim gold pen forming the numerals, Gabriel was very tempted to keep his big mouth shut.

Then, as he accepted the check she handed him, he spoke up. "I'm afraid you've made a slight error, Ms Whitfield. This is double my usual fee."

Eve appeared momentarily surprised. Gabriel could practically hear the wheels turning in her head as she made a decision. "This is what we routinely pay Owens and Martin; I see no reason why you shouldn't be worthy of an equal fee, Mr. Bouvier."

Gabriel decided that Ms Uptown Eve Whitfield was at her most appealing when she was struggling to be earnest. Actually, she was kind of cute. Suspecting that she wouldn't consider his masculine, undoubtedly chauvinistic observation a compliment, he wisely held his tongue.

"I appreciate your faith in my abilities," he said, matching her grave tone.

His expression was smooth, serious, but in the slanting rays of the late-afternoon sun, Eve caught a glint of laughter in his gleaming brown eyes. "Just see that you find Harry Keegan."

"Gabriel Bouvier always gets his man," he assured her with lazy humor. "I want to check out a few things that bother me about Keegan's yellow sheet. After that I'll need to speak to your mother."

"Yellow sheet?"

"The copy of Keegan's police record."

"Oh, that." She looked at the piece of paper on Gabriel Bouvier's desk as if it had just crawled out from beneath a particularly slimy rock.

"You see, Ms Whitfield, in order to find the guy, I need to know more about him than the fact that he's spent a lot of time dining in the state prison at the taxpayers' expense. I need to know where he likes to eat, favorite watering holes, what he does in his spare time."

"What spare time? From that report, the man seems to spend all his time either breaking into houses to steal jewels or serving time."

"Granted, Keegan's been busy. But he did manage to find time to court your mother," Gabriel pointed out.

"Only because she's lonely."

"It must be difficult being a widow."

"I suppose so." Eve agreed grudgingly. "Still, that isn't any reason for her to run off to the south of France with some professional thief."

"The south of France?"

"That's where they were planning to go on their honeymoon. Honeymoon," she repeated, heaping an extra helping of scorn on the word. "Can you imagine anything so ridiculous? For a couple their age?"

"I think it's kind of sweet."

"You would."

He folded his arms across his chest. "What exactly does that mean?"

Eve wondered what it was about the man that had made her speak out of turn. She was usually a great deal more circumspect. Her position as CEO of the Whitfield Palace Hotel chain demanded tact and diplomacy, neither of which she had demonstrated much of today.

"Your name, for one thing," she said reluctantly.

"What about it?"

Eve was fervently wishing she hadn't brought the subject up. "It's French."

"Cajun," he corrected. "So?"

Damn the man. He was baiting her, and loving every minute of it. Eve hated Gabriel Bouvier for being so intuitive even as she reminded herself that that was precisely why she was hiring him.

"Since you possess French ancestry, you're undoubtedly more romantic than the average man."

The corners of his mouth quirked in a grin. "Are you by any chance attempting to stereotype me, Ms Whitfield?"

"Not at all," she insisted, not quite honestly.

The truth was that Eve had always felt a bit more comfortable when she could categorize things. Including men. But try as she might, Gabriel Bouvier steadfastly refused to be labeled. The idea that he was like no other man she'd ever met was as intriguing as it was unsettling.

He nodded in satisfaction. "Good. Because I've never responded well to being shoved into pigeonholes. They're too confining, if you know what I mean."

Eve did but chose not to admit it. "You're not at all what I expected."

"Damn. Owens forgot to mention my fatal charm again."

She looked at him and shook her head. "Are you ever serious, Mr. Bouvier?"

"Only when necessary. Then I can be so serious it'd knock your socks off." His gaze moved from the smooth line of her thighs, visible beneath the white silk skirt, to her trim ankles. She had, Gabriel observed with masculine appreciation, very nice legs.

"What about your work?" she inquired, ignoring the spark of lust gleaming in his dark eyes as she recrossed her legs and adjusted her skirt. The movement allowed a flash of thigh.

Correction. She had great legs. Gabriel reluctantly returned his attention to her face. "I take my work very seriously, Ms Whitfield. Speaking of which, when can I meet your mother?"

From what she had seen of Gabriel Bouvier so far—his rugged dark looks and seemingly don't-give-a-damn attitude—he was precisely the type of man Dixie would find devastatingly appealing. A very strong part of Eve wanted to keep him as far away from her mother as possible.

Another, more pragmatic part knew that the man had a point. If anyone could give them clues concerning Harry Keegan's whereabouts, it would be the woman who'd spent three supposedly idyllic months with the man.

"Come to dinner tomorrow night," she decided, standing up. "We have cocktails at seven-thirty; you can talk to Dixie then."

Gabriel rose as well. "Fine. Where?"

Reluctantly she gave him an address in Audubon Place. "It's my parents' house," she insisted, at his smug expression. "So I'd appreciate it if you would refrain from any I-told-you-so remarks."

"I wouldn't think of it."

She gave him her coolest look. "I'll notify the guard at the St. Charles Avenue entrance that you'll be coming."

Her business settled, Eve was about to leave the office when something occurred to her. She turned, her hand on the antique brass doorknob. "We dress for dinner, Mr. Bouvier."

Gabriel grinned. "Why, thank you kindly for the warning, Ms Whitfield. Otherwise, I might have embarrassed both of us by turning up in the altogether."

He was, in a disturbing way, a very attractive man, with his jet-dark hair and nearly black fathomless eyes. He was wearing a white cotton shirt with the sleeves rolled up to just below the elbows, displaying his dark, well-muscled arms to advantage, and a pair of low-slung jeans. As she found herself suddenly imagining his lean, masculine body without clothing, soft color drifted into Eve's cheeks.

"I only mentioned it so you wouldn't feel uncomfortable."

The frost in her smoky voice didn't fool him for a second. She was definitely flustered. Gabriel had the distinct impression that there were very few things that could rattle the ever-so-proper Ms Whitfield. He decided that he rather liked being one of them.

"Thank you," he said gravely. "I appreciate your concern."

Eve eyed him with renewed suspicion, convinced that he was laughing at her again but unable to prove it.

"I'll see you tomorrow evening," he said, coming around the desk to see her out. As he took her arm, there was a jolt and a sudden flash of heat. Gabriel knew that he was not alone in experiencing the warmth tingling through his fingertips. Eve's face, as she stared up at him from behind the shield of those damn dark glasses, revealed astonishment.

There was a short, intense silence. Seconds ticked by as Eve struggled to regain her composure while her body throbbed with an almost overpowering sexual awareness.

"Tomorrow," she murmured distractedly. Then, unwilling to dwell on what had just occurred, Eve whirled around and fled down the wrought-iron stairway.

2

ONCE HE WAS ALONE, Gabriel picked up the telephone to dial the number he'd known for twelve years. It had just begun to ring on the other end when he changed his mind. Things like this were better done in person.

Leaving his office, he walked the short block and a half to Royal and Conti. The columned building he entered on the uptown river corner had been built in 1826 for the Bank of Louisiana. Today it housed the French Quarter police station. The air-conditioning was out, and everyone in the station—from the complainants to the suspects waiting to be booked to the uniformed cops—had one thing in common on this blistering July day. They all looked miserable. After the coolly proper Ms Whitfield, it came as a relief to see that some people, besides himself, still sweat.

"Tell me you've finally come to your senses and come back to work," Joe Reardon, Gabriel's former partner, greeted him. Reardon was a tall, lanky man with warm gray eyes and a friendly, calm disposition that brought to mind a Quaker farmer rather than a detective on a big city police force.

"What makes you think I'm not working?"

"Hell, we all know how you private dicks live. Fancy offices, fast cars, beautiful, grateful women falling into your bed day and night. You call that work?"

Gabriel had been having this conversation with his former partner for the past three years. They both knew it was a crock. "It's a dirty job—"

"—but somebody's got to do it," Reardon finished.

Gabriel glanced down at the stack of files piled on the floor beside Reardon's desk. "Looks as if you could use a little help."

"They keep promising to bring someone in to replace Murphy, but who the hell knows when that'll be," Reardon grumbled. "There's a budget crunch downtown; we might have to do without anyone to pick up the slack until after the end of the year."

The mention of Michael Murphy extinguished the smile lingering on Gabriel's face. Murphy had come to work at the precinct shortly before Gabriel had left the force. The kid had been bright, eager, and if a bit over-zealous, that was to be expected; in a lot of ways the new detective had reminded Gabriel of himself during his first months on the job. Perhaps that was the reason they'd become friends.

Three months ago Murphy had been conducting an investigation into an international jewel-theft ring operating in New Orleans. The quest had taken him to France after Paris police confiscated three pieces matching the description wired to Interpol after a burglary in the Garden District.

Michael Murphy, detective second class, had driven directly to the police station from Orly Airport, only to discover that the property department had misplaced the envelope with the jewelry. According to the Paris police reports, the duty officer had assured Murphy that the package would be located by the following day.

The detective never made it to his hotel. Five minutes after leaving the station, his taxi was rear-ended. When his driver leaped out of the cab to protest, a gunman stuck an automatic pistol into the open rear window and quite calmly and professionally pulled the trigger.

Remembering, both men frowned as they looked over at the desk Murphy had used. "Hey," Reardon said suddenly, trying to lighten the mood, "guess who floated to the surface of Lake Pontchartrain this morning?"

"Sounds like a trick question."

"Mad Max."

Gabriel whistled. Mad Max was a professional hit man reported to be every bit as crazy as he was lethal. "Any leads?"

"Not yet." Reardon grabbed for a piece of paper blown off the desk by the breeze from a nearby box fan. "But one popular train of thought is that somebody hired Mad Max to do a job, then hit him so he couldn't talk. Not that he would; say what you want, the guy was definitely a pro. But some people tend to get jumpy. So what favor do you want today?" he asked, pinning down another piece of paper.

"Can't a guy drop in and visit an old buddy?"

"Sure he can." He slammed an overflowing ashtray onto the stack of errant papers; ashes scattered over the top sheet, but Joe ignored the mess. "That's why you're carrying that yellow sheet."

"Now that you mention it, I would like to borrow your computer for a few minutes," Gabriel admitted.

"What do you want to know?"

"I'm interested in an arrest on New Year's Day, three years ago. Guy's name is Harry Keegan. He's supposed to have stolen a sixty-thousand-dollar sterling-silver Tiffany centerpiece from an antique shop on Royal owned by Mrs. Marie Gallier."

"That'd be on the central files."

"I've already got a copy of what's on the central files," Gabriel said. "What I'm looking for is a copy of the arresting officer's report."

Reardon pushed himself out of his chair. "Let's go see what we can scare up."

Fifteen minutes later they'd hit a dead end. Not only was there no arrest record for Harry Keegan in the files of the French Quarter precinct, there was also no record of any complaint filed by a Marie Gallier.

Gabriel would have been surprised if the files had turned up anything. By a stroke of luck, Mrs. Gallier owned the building that housed his office, and he knew she hadn't been burglarized at the time stated on Keegan's arrest record.

It had been his first month in business, and money had been even tighter then than it was now. When Mrs. Gallier had offered him a month's free rent in exchange for keeping an eye on her store while she was away visiting her sister, he'd jumped at the chance.

As Gabriel walked back to his office, he asked himself how Harry Keegan had managed to get himself sentenced to thirty-three months at the Louisiana State penitentiary on a nonexistent charge.

GABRIEL SPENT the following day talking to three individuals—one guard and two former inmates—who had been at the prison during Harry's alleged incarceration. None of them had ever heard of the guy.

As he drove out to Audubon Place that evening, Gabriel figured even Eve Whitfield would approve of his attire. He was wearing what he thought of as his FBI outfit: navy-blue suit, white shirt, red tie. Unfortunately, the temperature hadn't dropped more than two degrees from the day's record high, and by the time he got to Audubon Place, his suit was rumpled and limp. With a healthy pragmatism that had served him well for thirty-three years, Gabriel decided that you couldn't win them all.

As promised, the watchman in the guardhouse at Audubon Place had been told to expect him. Moments after his arrival, the large iron gate rumbled open, granting Gabriel admission to the most exclusive street in New Orleans.

The Whitfield mansion could easily have put Scarlett O'Hara's beloved Tara to shame. The large, two and a half story Greek Revival house was constructed of white stucco-covered brick, its facade shining like alabaster in the gleaming gold twilight. A raised parapet created an effect of added height while six massive Ionic columns supported the great roof. On either side of the main structure were single-story connecting wings that duplicated the mansion's architectural style. Unlike the Creole houses that crowded the sidewalk in the French Quarter, the mansions at Audubon Place were set far back from the street. A white wrought-iron fence surrounded a lushly manicured front lawn that could have doubled as a putting green.

In the center of the ornately carved oak door was an iron knocker fashioned in the shape of a horse's head.

Seconds after he'd knocked, the door was opened by an attractive woman dressed in a black uniform, white apron and starched white cap perched atop riotous auburn curls.

"Mr. Bouvier?" the maid inquired.

"That's me."

"Please come in, the family's waiting for you."

The interior of the Whitfield mansion was dominated by a massive entrance hall with Corinthian columns. A floating stairway curved up to the second floor, drawing a visitor's gaze toward a ceiling embellished with plaster medallions while underfoot white marble seemed to stretch on forever.

He'd just entered the house when a telephone began to ring; the maid glanced back and forth between the adjoining library and Gabriel, her dilemma obvious.

"Go ahead and answer it," he suggested. "I can find my own way."

"Thanks," she said with a sudden grin that made her appear a great deal less servile and several years younger. "Malcolm has a cold; I've been stuck doing double duty for the past two days."

"Malcolm?"

"The butler," she threw back over her shoulder as she hurried away to answer the telephone.

"Of course," Gabriel murmured. "How foolish of me not to have known."

"You'll find Dixie—Mrs. Whitfield, I mean, in the Gold Room. Fifth door on the left."

"Thanks."

As he approached the room, Gabriel heard voices. He remained in the hall, unabashedly eavesdropping.

"Tell me more about your Mr. Bouvier," a lush, throaty feminine voice requested.

"He's certainly not *my* Mr. Bouvier." Eve spoke this time. "And I've told you everything I know, Dixie."

"You haven't told me his birth date."

"Why on earth would you want to know the man's birth date?"

"I have my reasons," Dixie hedged.

"Oh, no," Eve groaned. "You've been to Madame Leblanc again, haven't you?" Madame Leblanc was an elderly woman who claimed to be a descendant of a famous old New Orleans voodoo queen. Her voodoo museum and gift shop—one of many in the city—was a French Quarter landmark.

"Something wrong with visiting an old friend?"

"When you and that old friend spend your time tossing chicken bones around, I'd have to say yes."

"We didn't toss any chicken bones around," Dixie insisted. "We merely talked."

"About Harry Keegan, I suppose."

"Of course. Madame says that you've done the right thing hiring Mr. Bouvier."

"Gee, I'm so pleased that she approved."

"Sarcasm doesn't suit you, dear," Dixie chided. "I don't suppose you'd happen to know if he had a birthmark," she suggested casually.

"A birthmark?"

"That's right. A small one at the base of his spine."

"Mother! I merely interviewed the man—I certainly didn't undress him."

"Don't worry, dear, I'll just have to ask him myself," Dixie decided.

"Why would you want to ask a total stranger something that personal?"

"Because Madame Leblanc says that Harry will be found by a man who has a small, crescent-shaped birthmark at the base of his spine. She also told me that the man with the birthmark is a Scorpio. I do wish we knew Mr. Bouvier's birth date."

"I hadn't realized that Madame Leblanc was also into astrology. Next you'll be telling me she's taken to using a crystal ball."

"I wouldn't be surprised—she's very versatile," Dixie said cheerfully. "Do you think your Mr. Bouvier could be a Scorpio?"

"For the second time, he is *not* my Mr. Bouvier." Eve glared down at her slim gold watch. "He's also late."

Gabriel checked his own watch; it was exactly seven thirty-one. "Good evening," he said, walking through the open doorway into a room every bit as ornately detailed as the entrance hall. "Sorry I'm late."

The room had the ambience of a baronial manner. Gilt-framed oil paintings hung on gold, silk-draped walls; satin-upholstered French period furniture rested on a Sarouk carpet. He recognized the pattern because there was one in the antique store below his office. The rug in the store had been priced at thirty thousand dollars; this one was at least twice as large.

"You're just on time, Mr. Bouvier," Dixie said with a welcoming smile. "Please come in—how delightful to meet you." She crossed the room, hands outstretched. Her full-skirted, bell-sleeved red taffeta dress rustled as she walked.

As he took the slender, beringed hands in his and looked down into her friendly face, Gabriel knew exactly what Eve was going to look like someday. Both women had glossy blond hair—in Dixie's case, it fell over her shoulders like a young girl's—high, slanting cheekbones, a slender nose, soft, inviting lips. Dixie's dark violet eyes reminded Gabriel that he'd yet to see Eve's.

"It's a pleasure to meet you, Mrs. Whitfield," he said, returning her smile with a warm one of his own. "Although I wish it could have been under more pleasant circumstances."

Dixie beamed as she patted his cheek reassuringly. "Don't worry—now that you're here, everything will turn out wonderfully. I know it."

She appeared so blissfully sure that Gabriel hesitated to pop her little bubble of contentment. Still, he had always prided himself on being straight with a client. "I'm glad you have such confidence in me, Mrs. Whitfield, but—"

"You must call me Dixie, dear," she interrupted cheerfully. "Everyone does. And what shall we call you?"

"Gabriel."

Her pansy-colored eyes brightened even more, and she clapped her hands with delight. "Gabriel! How remarkably interesting."

Gabriel shrugged. "I don't know how remarkable it is," he said. "The name's been in my family for generations. It's always been given to the firstborn son."

Dixie beamed. "Isn't that nice? Eve, dear," she said unnecessarily, "your guest is here."

Eve came toward him, as well, but not before Gabriel had witnessed the slight tensing of her shoulders. "Mr. Bouvier," she greeted him with a great deal less warmth than her mother had. "Thank you for coming." The air in the room was full of electricity—Eve could practically feel it arcing about her head.

Her eyes, framed by lashes that were surprisingly dark for someone with such fair hair, were a clear and startling blue. Lighter than her mother's, but no less compelling. She was wearing an ice-blue silk sheath that skimmed her slender body and gave her an elegantly glacial look. Her hair was in its customary bun at the back of her neck. Gabriel's fingers suddenly itched to pluck out the pins and run his fingers through the pale gold strands.

"You asked me to come," he reminded her, taking the hand she offered. He curled his long, dark fingers around hers, and as it had the first time he'd touched her, something hummed just beneath her skin, like an electric wire. This time there were no dark glasses to hide her shock of awareness as his thumb brushed the ultrasensitive skin of her palm.

"Yes. Well, now that you're finally here, I suppose we should get down to business," she said, practically jerking her hand free of his seductive touch.

"Fine," Gabriel said. *Later,* his dark eyes added.

Not on your life, Eve's blue eyes countered warningly.

"Wouldn't you care for a drink first, Gabriel?" Dixie asked brightly.

"Thanks. Bourbon would be great, if you have it."

"Of course we do. My husband always enjoyed his bourbon before dinner. Eve, since Marcie seems to have disappeared, could you please do the honors?"

"If Marcie's the maid, she had to answer the telephone," Gabriel said.

Dixie nodded knowingly. "She's getting married next week; it's been like a madhouse around here—caterers, florists, jewelers, travel agents...."

"Sounds like quite a bash," Gabriel said, wondering exactly how a maid could afford such an elaborate wedding.

"Dixie's orchestrating the affair," Eve explained. "As well as paying for it."

"Marcie's been like a daughter to me," Dixie said. "I don't know what I would have done without her, especially since Douglas's death. The girl is an absolute marvel," she told Gabriel. "She's taking a full load at Tulane with an A minus average, works six hours a day here, has a fiancé, and still makes time to talk to a lonely old lady."

"Fifty-six is certainly not old," Eve argued from the bar.

"Perhaps not," her mother agreed. "But I was lonely. Until Harry." She sighed heavily. "Dear, dear Harry." Dixie turned to Gabriel, putting her hand on his sleeve. Her nails, painted a deep red, gleamed like rubies. "You will find him, won't you, Gabriel?"

As he looked down into her violet eyes, which were presently pleading unashamedly, Gabriel suddenly understood the dilemma Eve was facing. It was obvious that Dixie was a warm, gentle woman who loved Harry Keegan a great deal. It also seemed obvious that the absent Harry Keegan was not exactly the retired business executive he had professed to be. So where did that leave Dixie? Or her daughter? Or himself, for that matter.

Gabriel patted the older woman's hand reassuringly. "I'll certainly do my best," he promised, exchanging a look with Eve. Guilt at what she proposed to do to scuttle her mother's romance flashed in her eyes for an instant, then she turned away.

"Please sit beside me and tell us all about yourself," Dixie said with an encouraging smile. "Eve mentioned that before opening your own agency, you were a police detective."

"I worked the Quarter for nine years," Gabriel said.

"Nine years. Goodness, you must have started at a very young age."

"I joined the force after graduating from LSU when I was twenty-one."

"And you've been a private detective for three years?"

"That's right."

"Which would make you thirty-three."

"Right again."

"And your birthday?"

"November twelfth."

"A Scorpio," Dixie said enthusiastically, exchanging a look with Eve. "Isn't that nice?"

"I wouldn't know," Gabriel said. "I don't read my horoscope."

"Oh, but you should," Dixie insisted. "Madame Leblanc says that—"

"Mother," Eve warned quietly.

"Yes, dear," Dixie said with a soft sigh.

Gabriel nodded his thanks to Eve, who'd placed a silver tray in front of him. The tray contained a cut-crystal decanter Gabriel suspected was Waterford, a matching glass, a bucket of ice and a bottle of bitters. Using sterling-silver tongs, he put some ice in the glass, added bitters, poured in some bourbon and took a sip.

Wild Turkey. Gabriel decided that besides the hefty fee, there were definite perks to working uptown.

"I've always loved the French Quarter," Dixie said. "Working there must have been quite a challenge."

"It was interesting."

Eve wondered why he'd quit if it was so interesting. But before she could ask, Marcie poked her curly auburn head in the door.

"Dinner's ready," the maid announced. "And Ethel says that if you don't all sit down right now, she isn't going to be responsible for what shape the food's in."

"Please tell Ethel we'll be right there, will you, Marcie?" Dixie instructed. "Gabriel, will you do me the honor of escorting me into the dining room?"

"Dixie," he said truthfully, "the honor is all mine."

They left the room, leaving Eve to follow.

3

THE DINING TABLE WAS COVERED in white damask and gleamed with an impressive display of silver, gold-rimmed china and crystal, which made Gabriel wonder if Harry Keegan, who'd surely sat at this table himself on more than one occasion, had managed to get his sticky fingers on any of the silverware before leaving town.

Dixie opened the conversation as Marcie served the first course, a cold tomato, basil and walnut soup. "You must lead a fascinating life."

"It would be exaggerating to say it's fascinating," Gabriel answered after taking a sip of the soup and finding it delicious. "But it does have its moments."

Dixie smiled approvingly at Eve. "He's modest," she pointed out. "I like that in a man. Despite his vast accomplishments, your father avoided becoming overly prideful. Harry's an incredibly modest man, too. Why, it takes a major effort to get him to say anything about his business."

"Don't I know that," Eve said under her breath.

"I was lucky to meet Harry after he'd retired," Dixie explained to Gabriel.

"Lucky," Eve murmured.

"Was his business in New Orleans?" Gabriel asked.

Dixie shook his head. "Oh, no. He's from Maine. Or Massachusetts." A puzzled frown marred the still-smooth line of her brow. "Or perhaps it was New Hampshire. Oh, dear, I always get those eastern states confused."

"Oh, everyone does," Gabriel assured her politely.

Dixie gave him a grateful look. There was a brief silence as everyone directed their attention to their soup. "I'm sorry I can't be more specific," she said after a time, "but he only mentioned it once. And then just in passing."

Gabriel nodded. "I understand."

"I know that wherever it was, it had a coastline," Dixie offered helpfully.

"How do you know that?"

"Because Harry loves to sail. He has a boat moored back there that he's going to have brought down to New Orleans. He's promised to teach me to sail. Then after our honeymoon we're going to take a trip to the Caribbean."

Eve's soup spoon stopped on the way to her mouth. "You didn't tell me anything about that."

"You didn't ask, dear," Dixie countered serenely. "And I was going to tell you. The very same night Harry disappeared."

"That's the night that he called and canceled your dinner engagement?" Gabriel asked.

"That's right. He said he had a family emergency."

"In Maine? Or wherever?"

"I'm sorry, Gabriel," Dixie apologized. "I really don't know. To tell you the truth, until that moment I didn't even know Harry had a family."

She fell silent as Marcie collected their empty bowls. A moment later the maid was back with mushroom and watercress salads.

Once everyone had been served, Dixie turned back
to Gabriel. "I realize that I sound horribly foolish,
agreeing to marry a man I don't appear to know anything about, but by the time you've reached my age,
you hope you've learned not to get bogged down in insignificant details. What was important was how we
felt about each other, not our individual net worth. Or
what work Harry had done before we'd met."

"How can you call a man's work an insignificant detail?" Eve challenged. "You know that Daddy lived for
Whitfield Palace Hotels."

"Of course I know that, Eve, dear," Dixie said. There
was a sharp edge to her usually quiet voice. "I am also
equally aware that Douglas died for Whitfield Palace
Hotels."

The sudden silence was deafening. Eve was the first
to break it. "I never realized that you resented the company."

Dixie's answering smile was somewhat wistful. "Of
course I didn't resent the company, darling. How could
I?" The girlish smile faded, and a touch of sadness appeared in her deep violet eyes. "I loved your father. I
could never have resented the single thing that meant
the most to him."

Shaking off the depressing thought, Dixie turned to
Gabriel, as if remembering her manners. "Bouvier," she
said in a bright, enthusiastic tone that Gabriel suspected was feigned. "It's Cajun, isn't it?"

"My family's from New Iberia," Gabriel confirmed
with a nod.

"Really?" Dixie asked with interest, obviously relieved to have the conversation turn away from herself. "What do they do there?"

"My mother runs a restaurant. She and my father started it together before I was born. Dad died a few years ago, but I've got plenty of cousins who help her out in the kitchen."

"How fascinating. Tell me, Gabriel, did your mother pass along any of her culinary skills to you? I've been wanting to learn how to cook Cajun cuisine for absolutely ages. But every time I attempt a recipe, Ethel—she's been our cook forever—accuses me of messing up her kitchen and chases me out."

"I've told you innumerable times that it's *your* kitchen," Eve reminded her mother tiredly. "Ethel works for you."

Dixie sighed. "I try to remember that, dear, but it's always a bit more difficult to remain firm when you're facing a three-hundred-pound woman brandishing a cleaver."

Gabriel threw back his head and laughed. "I'll make you a deal, Dixie," he offered. "Anytime you feel like messin' up a kitchen, just give me a call and you can come over and tackle mine."

"Really?"

"I ga-ron-tee." He drawled the familiar Cajun expression.

As Eve watched the pleasure flood into her mother's schoolgirl-bright eyes, she was forced to consider, not for the first time, that there was a chance she had misjudged Gabriel Bouvier.

Although Gabriel continued to question Dixie over a superbly prepared dinner of Lobster Savannah, carrots in brown sauce with fresh dill, stuffed summer squash and the tartest key lime pie he'd ever tasted, it was soon apparent that Harry Keegan had been purposefully vague when discussing his life. Other than a possible address near Lafayette Square, Eve's mother could provide little concrete information.

"WHAT ARE YOU going to do now?" Eve inquired as she walked with Gabriel toward the door. He'd already said his farewells to Dixie, promising to keep in touch.

Gabriel shrugged. "Start with the apartment, I suppose. The Irish Channel address Owens gave you turned out to be a dead end; I checked it out this morning. Keegan left there last month without leaving a forwarding address."

Her high heels made tapping sounds on the white marble. "You're going to this other apartment tonight?"

"No point in putting it off until tomorrow."

"It's not much, is it?"

He shrugged again. "It's a start."

"He's been gone for over a week. Won't the trail be terribly cold by now?"

"Trail?"

"Isn't that what you call it?"

He had to smile at her earnest expression. "Yeah. That's what we call it." Her hair smelled faintly of flowers. "You look nice tonight," he said. "I like that dress—the color matches your eyes."

She brushed at nonexistent wrinkles on the blue silk skirt. "Thank you. You look very nice, too."

It was the navy suit. It worked every time. Apparently even when wrinkled. "Thanks. I had a helluva time choosing which suit to wear."

"Oh, really? I didn't realize men worried about things like that."

"Sure we do. For instance, take tonight. I couldn't decide between this or the blue body stocking with the big red S on the front."

What happened next took him totally by surprise. Eve Whitfield smiled—a warm, dazzling smile that lit up her startling blue eyes. "That's a joke, isn't it?"

A dimple creased her cheek. He resisted the urge to taste it. "You're catching on, Ms Whitfield."

"I've been told that I'm quite bright."

"Of that I've not a single doubt. Tell your mother thanks again for the dinner. I'll check in with both of you tomorrow." He reached for the elaborately carved door handle.

"Just a minute," Eve said. "I'm coming with you."

Diplomacy had never been Gabriel's strong suit. "The hell you are."

"I'm paying you a very substantial fee, Mr. Bouvier. Therefore, I believe that I'm entitled to see firsthand what you discover in Harry Keegan's apartment."

Gabriel folded his arms over his chest. "In the first place, we don't even know if there's anything to find. And in the second place, Ms Whitfield, if I were willing to take orders, I would have remained in the police department."

Eve had lived with her father enough years to recognize male determination when she saw it. She immediately tried another tack. "I'm sorry—I shouldn't have put it quite that way."

"You shouldn't have put it that way," Gabriel agreed.

"It's just that all this has me so upset."

That he could believe. But her wide-eyed, syrup-sweet gaze was something else altogether. It looked like something he'd pour on his Sunday morning waffles. It was also phony as hell.

"Let's just skip the damsel-in-distress routine, okay? Unfortunately I left my suit of shining armor at home tonight, and if we want to get to the apartment house before the landlady hits the sack, we don't have time to run by my place and pick it up."

Eve was undeterred by his gritty tone. "You said we. Does that mean you're letting me come with you?"

"Do I have a choice?" Gabriel asked fatalistically.

She smiled again. It wasn't as breathtaking as the earlier one, but it stirred something inside him nevertheless. "I'm afraid not."

"I didn't think so," he grumbled. "Let's go."

A mercury-vapor floodlight illuminated the circular driveway, making the surroundings as bright as day. Eve stopped in front of Gabriel's three-year-old Plymouth.

"I thought private detectives all drove around in flashy sports cars."

"That's on television," he said, opening the passenger door for her. Gabriel knew that some radical feminists disapproved of such small acts of gallantry, but Eve appeared not to be one of them. He decided to be grateful for small mercies.

"I prefer to think of myself along the lines of Lamont Cranston," he continued after getting in the driver's side. "Using my anonymity to cloud men's minds."

"Lamont Cranston?" Eve asked vaguely as she struggled with what appeared to be a hopelessly tangled seat belt.

"Yeah. 'Who knows what evil lurks in the hearts of men? The Shadow knows.' Lamont Cranston . . . from the old radio program." He groaned at her blank expression. "Don't tell me you haven't heard it."

"Sorry."

"That's okay. The point I was trying to make was that in my line of work, it's important to blend in. To avoid being noticed."

He reached over to help her untangle the twisted seat belt. When his arm accidentally brushed against her breasts, Eve drew in a quick breath at the tension suddenly coiling inside her. Her chest tightened.

"I think I'd notice you."

The atmosphere was thick with sexual awareness. As she stared up at him, confusion and desire warring in the sapphire depths of her eyes, Gabriel found himself sorely tempted.

"Would you really?"

"Really," she said in a soft, inviting tone that surprised both of them.

Deciding that this was not the time to dwell on this unexpected development, Gabriel turned away from temptation and turned the key in the ignition with hands that were not as steady as they should have been.

"We'd better get going," he said. "Before the trail gets any colder."

Neither Gabriel nor Eve appeared inclined toward conversation as they passed through the heavy wrought-iron gates of Audubon Place and headed toward Lafayette Square. During the prolonged silence Eve forced herself to face the fact once again that Gabriel aroused dangerous feelings in her. Feelings that were far too risky for her own good.

Lafayette Square had once been the political center of New Orleans, and although in recent years the square had become home for skid-row derelicts, a concerted effort was being made to restore the area to its former grandeur. Surrounded by federal buildings, the grounds had been beautifully planted, but Gabriel thought that the benches occupied by sleeping winos detracted a bit from the square's charm.

Harry Keegan's apartment was located in a building on a street undergoing ambitious residential renovation. Red-brick townhouses dating from the 1830s, in demand by yuppies who had no intention of following their parents to the suburbs, shared the block with seedy tenements and service shops. An abandoned building Gabriel knew to be a crack house was across the street from a recently restored office building housing a trio of law firms.

The narrow street was teeming with people driven outdoors by the heat. The neighborhood kids had knocked the top off a nearby fire hydrant and were playing in the cool, gushing cascade while the adults looked on enviously.

When Gabriel pulled up in front of Harry Keegan's apartment building, he instructed Eve to remain in the car.

"Don't be silly. I'm coming in with you."

"The hell you are."

"Despite what you may consider my rarefied upbringing, I am far from being a hothouse flower, Mr. Bouvier. I will not wilt in the face of poverty. Or adversity."

"Good for you. So why don't you prove it by not wilting in the car."

"I'd prefer to come with you."

Gabriel wondered what it would be like to go through life getting precisely what he wanted. "Look, it's my job to watch out for you, and I'd prefer that you didn't. And since I'm the one in charge of this little expedition, what I say goes. Okay?" He pulled the keys from the ignition and pocketed them.

"No."

"What did you say?" Deciding that the occasion called for decisive action, he gave her the long, hard look he'd developed over the years of working the streets. While not overtly threatening, he'd been assured that it was decidedly intimidating.

Eve had no doubt that Gabriel had experienced his share of violence. The deeply etched lines bracketing his mouth and fanning out from his dark eyes were proof of that. At the same time, however, a deep-seated instinct assured her that he was not the type of man who'd ever harm a woman. Such knowledge allowed her a feeling of serene self-confidence.

"I said no." To Gabriel's irritation, Eve did not appear to be quaking in her high heels as she returned his practiced glare with a level look of her own. "In case you've forgotten, Mr. Bouvier, I hired you to find Harry Keegan. Not to live out your adolescent macho fantasies."

"My what?" Frustration mixed with irritation flashed dangerously in his dark eyes. Some of the older children had stopped running through the water and were standing on the curb, eyeing them with interest. Their sitting in the car was attracting attention, which Gabriel had wanted to avoid.

"You heard me."

"I heard you," Gabriel agreed gruffly. "I just don't know what the hell you're talking about."

"Don't you? Are you trying to tell me that you weren't playing the role of the white knight? The big strong man protecting the weak dependent female?"

Now the adults were watching them, as well. Gabriel was beginning to feel as if he and the argumentative Eve Whitfield were in a goldfish bowl. He didn't like the feeling. Not one damn bit. "Look, Eve, I'll admit to being concerned for your safety," he continued gravely. "If that makes me a chauvinist, I'm sorry, but that's the way I feel. I'd also like to know one thing."

"What?"

"Would you have come here tonight alone?"

"Of course not," she responded immediately.

"But you did agree to come along with me."

Eve knew exactly where he was going with this particular line of questioning. "Yes," she muttered reluctantly.

"So the case could be made that you were counting on my protection."

"You think you have me all figured out, don't you?"

"No," he said honestly. "But I will."

She looked him in the eye. "Are you always this sure of yourself?"

She intrigued him even as she irritated the hell out of him. Gabriel tried to remind himself that he'd always enjoyed a challenge. "No. Are you always this argumentative?"

She allowed a slight smile. "No."

"Perhaps we just bring out the best in one another," he said, putting an end to the conversation as he opened the door and got out of the car. He didn't bother protesting as Eve followed. Lightning flashed on the horizon, an erratic, jagged streak that split the sky.

"Hey," he called out to a young boy who looked to be around eleven.

"Yeah?" he asked with exaggerated uninterest.

Realizing that the kid was unimpressed by his navy suit, Gabriel pulled a bill out of his pocket. "How about watching my car while we visit a friend?"

"Sure, man. Hey, for ten I'll even wash it."

"That's not necessary. But thanks, anyway."

"It's your heap. You want it to look like a mudball, I guess that's your business." The kid shrugged as he stuffed the bill into the spandex waistband of his swimming trunks.

"You should have sprung for the ten," Eve advised as they approached the building.

"Hey, if you don't like my car, why don't you just come out and say so?"

A man dressed in a pair of blue shorts and a sleeveless white undershirt was sitting on the steps of Harry Keegan's apartment building.

"Evening," Gabriel greeted him, receiving a grunt in return. "We're looking for the manager."

"You a cop?"

Gabriel shook his head. "No."

"You look like a cop."

"People say that all the time; I think it's the suit." Gabriel took a scuffed leather wallet from his back pocket. The folder, which he opened for the man, contained his license and gun permit.

"So you're a *private* cop," the man said. "Not a helluva lot of difference." His gaze shifted to Eve. "'Cept cops usually don't run around with such good-lookin' broads."

Gabriel could practically feel the rumblings emanating from deep inside Eve like Vesuvius just before she blew. "The manager?"

The man jerked his head toward the front door. "Apartment 1-A. Can't miss it."

"Thanks."

The man didn't answer. Neither did he seem inclined to move. Eve and Gabriel had to step around him as they went up the stairs.

The thick, moist air inside the building was redolent with cooking smells, stale sweat and mildew.

"Sure you don't want to wait in the car?" Gabriel asked.

Eve took a deep breath. "Positive."

"I'll say this for you, lady, you're a glutton for punishment." He shook his head in a mixture of frustration and admiration as he knocked on the door of apartment 1-A. A television blared in the background.

The woman who answered the door was in her mid-fifties. Her blond hair was dyed a color that reminded Gabriel of Fritos; a cigarette hung from between her lips.

"Yeah?" She seemed no more impressed with his suit than anyone else in the neighborhood.

"Good evening, ma'am," Gabriel said in his best Sergeant Joe Friday voice. "I'm Gabriel Bouvier, and this is my, uh, associate, Ms Eve Whitfield."

"Good for you. So what?" The cigarette bobbed as she talked.

He flipped open the license once again, revealing the laminated card with the photo in the upper left-hand corner. "I'm a Louisiana State licensed investigator—"

"A private dick, huh?"

"Investigator," Gabriel corrected, ignoring Eve's faint smile.

The woman shrugged. "Same thing. So what do you and Princess Di here want with me?"

Once again Gabriel felt Eve struggling to control her escalating temper. She was the one who had insisted on coming here tonight; she couldn't say he hadn't warned her.

"We're looking for Harry Keegan."

"Well, you're looking in the wrong place. He ain't been here all week."

"He moved out?" Eve was visibly stricken by the news.

The woman gave her a long look. "Did I say he'd moved out?"

"Well, no, but—"

"I said he ain't been here. Since he only took one measly suitcase, I figure he'll be comin' back sooner or later."

"You saw him leave?" Gabriel asked.

"Why is it," the landlady said to Eve, "that the good-looking ones are always so god-awful dumb?"

"I suppose that's nature's way of evening things out," Eve answered.

The woman nodded. A long gray ash fell unnoticed to the scuffed linoleum floor. "Mebee. Anyway," she said, directing her words back to Gabriel, "if I didn't see Harry leave, how'd I know he was carrying a valise?"

"Good point. When was that?"

"Last Wednesday. I know 'cause I was watching out the window, waiting for my check to come from the county."

"And you haven't heard from him since?"

"Nope. But his rent runs out on the first. If he hasn't paid it, I'm confiscating every piece of junk he's got up there." She glared at Gabriel defiantly. "It says I can in his lease."

"Sounds reasonable to me," he agreed, knowing full well that there was no lease. "Could we take a look at his room?"

"That'd be trespassing. Long as his rent's paid."

"We're friends of his," Gabriel said.

"Exactly how friendly are you?"

"Ten dollars' worth?"

"I'd be more inclined to look the other way for twenty."

Gabriel pulled another bill from his wallet. The twenty disappeared into the top of the woman's dingy nylon slip. "Apartment 5-E." She closed the door before he could request the key.

"Princess Di, indeed," Eve fumed as they began climbing the stairs.

"You could take it as a compliment."

Eve's only response was an unladylike grunt.

By the time they'd reached the third-floor landing, she was grateful for her aerobics classes. She hoped Gabriel had noticed that she wasn't out of breath.

"Do you have to keep handing out all that money?" she complained as they continued up the dimly lighted stairwell.

"You agreed to pay me a daily fee plus expenses. What did you think the expenses consisted of?"

"I don't know. Telephone calls. Gasoline. Lunch, maybe."

"I can afford to pay for my own lunch, thank you. And gas comes out of the daily fee unless I have to go out of town. Then you'll be billed mileage. You spring for long-distance calls, pay phones, bribes and bullets."

"Bullets?"

"In case I have to shoot anyone in the line of duty."

He was only kidding, but Eve didn't seem to realize that. Her expression, as she looked up at him, was solemn. "Have you ever shot anyone, Gabriel?"

He was suddenly wishing he hadn't brought the subject up. "Yeah."

"When you were a policeman?"

"Yeah."

They'd stopped under one of the few ceiling lights in the ramshackle building that hadn't been broken. Her wide blue eyes searched his face. "You didn't enjoy it."

"No."

She nodded, sober but satisfied. "I knew it."

"Knew what?"

"That underneath that rough, obnoxious exterior was a nice man."

"Yeah," he drawled. "I'm a regular sweetheart."

4

THE LOCK HAD obviously been forced. After checking to make certain that Eve was where he'd left her by the stairwell, Gabriel put his ear to the door. Nothing. Standing to one side, he slowly turned the knob.

It was a small efficiency apartment—no foyer, just a living room-bedroom combination with what an overly optimistic rental agent might describe as a galley kitchen along one wall, if a portable refrigerator and a hot plate could be considered a kitchen. There was a bathroom the size of a broom closet adjoining the room; it was there Gabriel found the body.

The man—broad shoulders, iron-gray crew cut, chin like a shovel scoop—was lying on his back. There was a gaping hole in his chest.

Gabriel shook his head in an unconscious gesture of regret. Harry Keegan wouldn't be sailing to the Caribbean anytime soon. Neither would he be eloping with Dixie Whitfield to the south of France. It looked as though someone else had just solved Eve Whitfield's little family problem.

He was on his way out of the apartment when he almost ran into Eve, who was on her way in. He took hold of her arm. "I thought I told you to stay put."

"I was worried about you."

"I'm fine. Let's get out of here."

He was standing between Eve and the open bathroom door. She tried to look past him into the apartment. "Did you find anything?"

"Yeah. Let's go. I've got a call to make."

"You didn't spend very much time looking around," she complained. "How could you have searched the apartment that fast?"

"It's a small apartment."

"What did you find?"

"I'll tell you downstairs."

The grim expression on his face gave him away. His hold on Eve wasn't very firm, making it a simple matter for her to pull away and go around him.

"Oh, my God." At the sight of the dead man lying only a few feet away in a pool of dark blood, her head began to spin. She choked back the scream that rose in her throat.

"Dammit, I told you to stay put." Gabriel pulled her out into the hallway. "Take some deep breaths."

Eve did as instructed, exhaling in painful, shuddering gasps. When her head began to clear, she looked up at Gabriel.

"Who do you think it is?" Her face was pale, and horror still swirled in her eyes. "You don't think Harry could have killed him, do you?"

Gabriel wondered if the sudden shock had done something to her mind. "Eve, I know you didn't expect things to end like this, but that *is* Harry Keegan."

"No." She shook her head. "No," she repeated, a bit more firmly this time. "It's not Harry."

"Are you sure?"

"Positive. He looks a lot like Harry—same haircut, same build and age—but it's not him . . . That call you have to make . . . it's to the police, isn't it?"

"Yes."

Her expression was bleak. "Harry's in a great deal of trouble, isn't he, Gabriel?"

Gabriel wanted to take her into his arms and assure her that whatever happened he'd keep her safe. That what had happened to that stranger would never— could never—happen to her. That he'd find Harry Keegan, wherever he was, pay the guy off and that would be the end of it.

"Yes," he answered instead. "I think he is."

IT HAD FINALLY BEGUN to rain; huge drops pelted down on the sizzling asphalt. Some of the people in the crowd gathered on the sidewalk had their faces directed skyward, reveling in the feel of the cool water on their skins. Others watched the activity going on outside the red-brick apartment building with grim satisfaction. The flashing blue and red bubble lights of the patrol cars were reflected in the rain-slick street while men in blue uniforms or dark suits went in and out of the building.

Eve sat alone in the Plymouth, her arms wrapped around her body as she watched Gabriel talking to the detectives. She felt numb, strangely removed from the scene. It was almost as if a surrealistic film was unfolding in front of her. Raindrops spattered the windshield.

"You've had a busy day," Joe Reardon commented as he stood in the doorway of the building with Gabriel.

Upstairs, the mobile-laboratory technicians were dusting the apartment for prints. The medical examiner was conducting a preliminary, cursory examination of the body while the police photographer complained to anyone who would listen about being called away from his twenty-fifth wedding anniversary party.

Gabriel shrugged. "No more than usual."

"Don't be so modest." Reardon pulled a pack of cigarettes from his suit pocket, shook one loose, stuck it between his lips and lit it with a red plastic lighter. "First a morning visit to the state prison—"

"I was visiting a friend."

"Who just happens to be a guard."

"That's right."

"A guard who was working during the time Harry Keegan, who I had never heard of until yesterday when you asked me to run a check on him, was incarcerated."

"Allegedly incarcerated," Gabriel corrected. "But I can't find anyone who remembers his being an inmate during that time."

"That explains the afternoon visit to Joey the Ferret."

"Joey was in for loan-sharking a couple years ago."

Reardon exhaled a cloud of smoke. "And?"

"He's never heard of Keegan."

"It's a big prison. People come and go."

"And Joey's got a line on everyone in it—who else do you know whose business actually triples when he's sent up?"

"Maybe Keegan's a customer. Joey didn't get where he is today by ratting on his clientele."

"Could be, but something's still screwy about all this."

"Like?"

"Like this Keegan guy is some kind of phantom—he doesn't exist."

"That stiff upstairs looks pretty damn real for a phantom."

"The guy upstairs isn't Keegan."

Reardon gave him a sharp look. "You sure about that?"

"Positive."

"I don't suppose you'd care to give me your source for that enlightening information?"

Gabriel shook his head as Reardon's speculative gaze moved to the woman curled up in the front seat of the Plymouth. "You know I can't, Joe. But if I knew the identity of the guy upstairs, I'd sure as hell give it to you."

"The lab guys said he's clean," Reardon grumbled. "We'll run the fingerprints—something's bound to come up."

"I'll call you in the morning."

Joe Reardon studied him thoughtfully through the blue haze between them. "What's your interest in all this, anyway?"

"Sorry. I can't talk about it. Not yet."

The detective's eyes were still fixed on Eve. "Either your social life has taken a quantum leap, or you're working for the Whitfields."

"Ms Whitfield and I have been out dancing," Gabriel lied easily.

"Sorry I bothered to ask."

"Really. She likes the way I dip."

"Yeah, I can tell you've impressed the hell out of her. Why don't you do the gentlemanly thing and get the lady out of here? Oh, and tell your client we'll need to talk with her tomorrow."

"Come on, Reardon. She doesn't know anything about this."

"Then I shouldn't have to take up much of her time."

"Just enough to get her name splattered all over the papers."

The detective shrugged as he dropped the cigarette and ground it into the wet pavement with his heel. "It's not that big a story—just another skid row murder. There's no reason for the press to know anything about Ms Whitfield's role in discovering the body."

"Sometimes you amaze me with your sensitivity, Joe."

"Yeah, I'm a real prince of a guy. Oh, one more thing, Bouvier..."

Gabriel stopped in the process of opening the car door. "What's that?"

"When are you going to get a new suit? That one looks like you took it off one of those winos over in Lafayette Square."

Gabriel's brief, answering gesture politely suggested the detective return to work.

"WHERE DO YOU LIVE?" Gabriel asked as he pulled the Plymouth away from the curb.

Eve was staring out the passenger window into the night, but she wasn't seeing the rain-washed street. She was seeing that dead man in Harry Keegan's apartment. With his eyes— Oh, God, those wide, unfocusing eyes.

"Eve?" Gabriel said gently.

She didn't turn her head. "Yes?"

"Where do you live?"

"Why?" Her voice was flat. Expressionless.

"I'm taking you home," he replied.

"But I left my car at Dixie's."

"Someone can pick it up tomorrow."

She sighed. "I suppose you're right. I live at Pont-chartrain Vistas. It's a condominium. On Lakeshore Drive."

"I know where it is."

Silence settled over the interior of the car. There was only the sound of the rain pelting down on the metal roof. Despite New Orlean's reputation as a late-night city, they were almost alone on the street. A dark, late-model sedan followed discreetly half a block behind the Plymouth; every so often another car would pass them, going in the opposite direction.

Gabriel knew that Eve would need to talk about tonight, but he decided to wait until the shock wore off. All the same, he was amazed that she was handling the situation as well as she was. Perhaps her cool, calm demeanor was not as feigned as he'd first thought.

But then he remembered those intriguing flashes of temper. And wondered.

Eve was grateful for Gabriel's lack of conversation. Her brain felt strangely numb, although a maniac was pounding away inside her head with a jackhammer. Her stomach felt as if it were riding a roller coaster.

The man in Harry Keegan's apartment was not the first dead person she'd seen. Her father had died in her arms. But as horrific as that experience had been, it was not the same. After asking her to take care of the company and Dixie, Douglas Whitfield had appeared amazingly calm, given the circumstances. Even peaceful. The man in Harry's apartment had died fighting. The revolver clutched in his lifeless hand was proof of that.

The unwelcome image lingered before her eyes. Eve moaned softly and pressed her fingertips against her closed lids. Without taking his attention from his driving, Gabriel reached over and took her hand in his.

They continued that way for three blocks, their linked hands on the seat between them, neither saying a word. The street remained, for the most part, deserted. Only that single car continued to follow them.

Gabriel turned left at the corner.

The car followed.

Gabriel went another two blocks, then made a right turn on the red light.

So did the dark sedan.

Watching carefully in his rearview mirror, Gabriel cursed.

The grim oath captured Eve's attention. She glanced over at Gabriel. He was strikingly alert, his profile as rigid as stone.

"What's wrong?"

"Don't turn around, but we've got company."

Her stomach flipped before plunging. "Company?"

"Company. The uninvited kind."

He released his hold on her hand to reach into the glove compartment, retrieving a .38-caliber revolver. The gun had a steel-blue finish and a walnut stock with an S&W monogram. It was the first gun Eve had ever seen up close. She hoped it would be the last.

"Get down," Gabriel instructed brusquely as he suddenly punched the gas pedal to the floor. Eve was pressed against the back of the seat as the car took off like a rocket. "And stay there until I tell you it's safe to sit up."

Not needing a second invitation, Eve slumped down low, closed her eyes, gripped the edge of the seat with frozen fingers and began to say a number of small silent prayers as they sped through the dark, quiet streets, the car's engine roaring and its tires squealing on the wet pavement.

From Gabriel's periodic curses Eve knew that whoever was following them was still there. Every so often the wheels of the car would go over a curb, causing her stomach to lurch even more. She opened her eyes just in time to watch in terror as Gabriel twisted the steering wheel, swerving into the opposite lane to avoid a large, slow-moving truck on its way to the produce market with a load of melons. Another truck, this one a gasoline tanker, was headed directly toward them. Eve's heart was in her throat as Gabriel deftly piloted the Plymouth between the two trucks with inches to spare.

"That was," she said, once her heart rate began returning to normal, "very impressive."

The maneuver had effectively blocked off the sedan. Gabriel allowed himself to relax. For now. "Thanks," he said, giving her a slight grin. "You can sit up now."

Emboldened by his change in mood, Eve allowed herself a glance behind them. "They're gone?"

"For the time being."

"Who do you think it was?"

"That's a little difficult to tell at this point."

It was still raining. The wipers were sweeping back and forth across the windshield, clearing the water off in fan-shaped sheets. Lightning arced over the tall buildings; thunder boomed.

"Do you think whoever it was had something to do with that man's death?"

"I wouldn't be surprised."

"Which would mean they also have something to do with Harry. Since the man *was* killed in Harry's apartment."

"Could be."

Eve leaned her head against the passenger window. The glass was cool against her skin. "I think I'm beginning to hate this."

"You could always call it quits," Gabriel suggested, even as he wondered if it wasn't a bit too late for that. Whoever had been tailing them had undoubtedly been watching the apartment, which meant they'd seen Eve. If they knew who she was . . .

"No." The look she gave him echoed her softly spoken denial. Her eyes were filled with a mixture of lingering shock and fear. But there was no mistaking the determination in their depths. "If Harry is involved in something illegal or dangerous, that's all the more reason to find him. Before he drags Dixie into whatever it was that got that man killed."

They were passing City Park. Inside was a stand of trees called the Dueling Oaks because of the many sunrise duels once fought there. To the proud Creoles of early New Orleans, nothing—not even death—had been so dreaded as a loss of honor. Studying Eve's serious expression, Gabriel had the feeling she had more than a nodding acquaintance with the idea of maintaining family honor.

It was obvious that she was scared. It was also readily apparent that she was doing her best to hide it. Cool steel swathed in smooth and gleaming silk—that was Eve Whitfield. She was proving a difficult woman to resist, and for a fleeting moment Gabriel wondered why a man would even want to.

"Your mother's a lucky woman," he said.

She stubbornly fought off rising waves of nausea. "You can still say that, even when you don't approve of my plan to buy Harry Keegan off?"

"I never said I didn't approve."

"You never said you did, either."

That was true enough. At this moment Gabriel couldn't have honestly said how he felt about Eve's plan. Because nothing about this case was turning out to be simple.

"I know you'll do the right thing," he said after a brief, thoughtful pause. "Whatever that turns out to be."

Realizing that she had just received a vote of confidence from a man she doubted handed out compliments very often, Eve told herself that she should have felt encouraged by his words. But try as she might, she couldn't get that dead man out of her mind.

Pontchartrain Vistas was a modern glass building, offering its affluent residents unparalleled views of the lake. Gabriel doubted that he could have afforded the monthly maintenance fee, let alone what buying an apartment in the building must cost. He pulled into the visitors' parking lot and cut the engine.

"I'll walk up with you."

Eve nodded. "Thank you." She frowned as she watched him tuck the revolver into his belt. "Do you have to take that with you?"

"Yes."

"I don't like guns."

"If those guys who were tailing us come back, you might find yourself liking them a little better," he suggested.

"You can't just walk past the doorman wearing a gun. It'll look like something out of Dodge City. The shoot-out at the O.K. Corral."

"The shoot-out at the O.K. Corral was in Tombstone."

"You know what I mean. What will he think?"

"Perhaps he'll think I'm trying to keep you alive," he answered quietly.

Eve's already pale complexion blanched to chalk white as she stared at him. "Surely you don't really think—"

"At this point I don't know what to think," he cut in brusquely. "All I know is that I'm not about to take any chances." His tone softened. "I'll button my jacket. The doorman will never notice."

Eve didn't know which she found more disconcerting: the fact that she was in the company of a man wearing a gun, or the fact that said man believed her life might be in danger.

"Thank you," she said softly.

"Anything to keep a client happy."

From the interested look the liveried doorman gave him as he entered the building with Eve, Gabriel got the distinct impression that it was unusual for her to arrive home late at night with a man in tow. For some reason, which he wasn't going to take time to examine at the moment, Gabriel found the idea undeniably appealing.

If he'd expected her apartment to give him any surprising insights into Eve's personality, Gabriel would have been highly disappointed. The place mirrored the self-controlled image she presented to the world. White predominated: alabaster walls, snowy carpeting, a white modular sofa and matching chairs. White blinds covered the windows. Brass—cachepots, candlesticks—provided gleaming color more cold than bright.

Unlike his own apartment, no magazines cluttered nearby tables; no dirty glasses marred the gleaming white marble mantle. There was no clutter, no mess, not a speck of dust. From what he could see, everything was absolutely, positively perfect. Gabriel felt something akin to claustrophobia.

He could feel her watching him and knew some comment was in order. One look at her ashen face told him that conversation could wait.

"Eve, are you—"

Her stomach, which had been roiling for the last half hour, suddenly lurched. She pressed her palm against her lips. "I'm sorry," she said, escaping the room.

Not bothering to ask if she wanted company, Gabriel followed, holding her head while she lost the rich dinner Dixie's cook had prepared. When she'd finally finished retching, he dampened a white washcloth and, crouching beside her, moved it over her face. Her exquisitely smooth skin was cold and clammy.

"Feeling better?"

Eve began to nod, then wished she hadn't. Her head throbbed. She leaned back against the tile wall and closed her eyes. "I think so. I'm sorry."

"For what?"

"For behaving like a hysterical female."

Her lashes were dark against her pale cheeks. And she was trembling. At this moment Eve looked a great deal younger than the twenty-nine Gabriel knew her to be. And much more fragile. She stirred something deep inside him. Something alien and entirely unexpected. Gabriel told himself that it was merely an understandable desire to protect her.

"Eve, you were far from hysterical. As for getting sick, if it makes you feel any better, I threw up after seeing my first body, too."

She opened her eyes and looked directly into his. "Did you really?"

"Yes." He ran the cool cloth over her cheekbones. Her color was slowly returning.

"But then you got used to it?"

Gabriel shook his head. "No. You never get used to it. Oh, you learn to stomach the physical impact. You can't continue to do your job if you don't learn to deal with that. But believe me, sweetheart, you never get so jaded that you remain unaffected by the senseless taking of a life."

His expression turned grim as he thought about the young and optimistically enthusiastic Michael Murphy. Now there had been a tragic, senseless loss.

Admiration flickered in the depths of Eve's wide blue eyes. "Thank you."

Gabriel shrugged off her whispered words of gratitude. "Hey, it's the truth."

A few blond hairs had escaped the intricate twist at the back of her neck, causing Gabriel to wonder what she'd look like with her hair loose and blowing in a soft summer breeze. That provocative image led to yet another, one where her love-tousled hair was strewn wantonly over his pillow. Or his chest.

He tucked the errant strands behind his ear, allowing his fingers to linger. Beneath his fingertips he felt her pulse increase its beat.

"You know, you really did behave like a trooper back there."

His light touch was warming the skin behind her ear in a way that was as intriguing as it was disconcerting. As his hand trailed down her throat, Eve drew in a quick, deep breath but didn't relax.

"I felt as if I was going to faint," she admitted.

Gabriel didn't take his eyes from hers. "But you didn't. And you didn't scream once when I was trying to ditch that car."

She smiled faintly. "Actually, if you want the unvarnished truth, I found that part rather exciting."

Gabriel smiled in return. "Ah, underneath the composed exterior the lady has a secret taste for danger."

Eve considered his words. "Perhaps I do, at that."

"You sound surprised."

"I believe I am."

Surprised was hardly the word for it. Douglas Whitfield had drilled self-control into Eve from an early age, reminding her that emotionalism had no place in the business world. First father, then daughter had waged a battle against an impulsive streak inherited from Dixie. Eve had thought she'd long since conquered the trait that her larger-than-life father had always viewed as a distressing character flaw. Now she was forced to wonder.

Gabriel chuckled. "Think of it as one of the many lagniappes you receive when you're clever enough to choose me over all the other private investigators in the city."

A lagniappe was a New Orleans expression meaning something extra, something not paid for. Like the thirteenth doughnut when you ordered a dozen. Well, so far she had definitely gotten more than she expected when she'd hired Gabriel Bouvier.

"You didn't mention the lagniappe when we spoke yesterday," she said.

"I'm just full of surprises." Reaching down, he took her hand, pulling her gently to her feet. "That's one of my many charms. You'll want to brush your teeth. Why don't I make us a drink? I think we could both use one."

Although her head had ceased to swim, Eve wasn't certain she could handle anything alcoholic. "You're welcome to help yourself, but I think I'd rather have a cup of tea."

"I'll have it ready in a jiffy."

"You don't have to do that."

"No problem—just think of it as yet another lagniappe." He left the room before she could answer.

Eve brushed her teeth, gargled with peppermint-flavored mouthwash, washed her face and repinned the loose hairs that Gabriel had tucked behind her ear. Feeling a great deal more human, she returned to the living room.

She could hear Gabriel banging around in the kitchen. At first she considered joining him, then, realizing that she was suddenly incredibly weary, she sank down onto the white sofa, tucked her legs under her and stared out over the moon-gilded waters of Lake Pontchartrain. The rain had stopped, and the clouds had blown out into the gulf. The night was clear, the deep purple sky filled with stars.

From this viewpoint Eve could see the Mardi Gras fountain spraying its cascading tower of water into the air. Lights—purple for justice, green for faith and gold for power—danced through the rising water, creating a colorful effect. Usually the scene gave her pleasure. But not tonight. Not after all that had happened.

"I didn't know which kind you'd want," Gabriel said as he returned to the room with a gray mug in his hands. "So I decided on the chamomile; my grandmother claims it's a balm for just about anything."

She smiled her thanks as she took the mug. "Chamomile's fine. Your grandmother's still alive?"

"Yeah. Actually, both my grandmothers are still alive. Grandmère Bouvier is in her seventies and still working her sugarcane field. Thirty-five years ago the farm bureau sent a man out to her place to explain that Louisiana's climate isn't really right for sugarcane. But we're a stubborn people, we Cajuns. And we believe in tradition. So my grandmother continues to plant her sugarcane every year, never minding that every four or five years an early freeze causes a bad crop."

Eve sipped the soothing tea. "She sounds wonderful."

"She is." Gabriel's smile revealed his affection for the elderly woman. "Sure you don't mind if I have a drink?"

Eve waved toward a nearby chrome-and-glass trolley laden with crystal decanters. "Help yourself. Tell me about your other grandmother."

Gabriel had the feeling that at any other time Eve might not be so fascinated by his family tree. It was obvious that she wanted to talk about something, anything, to keep her mind off what she'd been through this evening.

"Grandmère Courrege is my mother's mother; she's a *traiteur*," he said, going over to the portable bar and pouring some Courvoisier into a balloon glass.

Observing him over the rim of her mug, Eve admitted to herself that Gabriel Bouvier was a very attractive man. Especially when he smiled. If she didn't watch herself, she'd be tempted to forget that her relationship with the man was strictly business. The business of locating Harry Keegan.

"A *traiteur*?"

He took a sip of the expensive cognac and nodded appreciatively. It was as smooth as velvet, creating a comfortable warmth as it went down. "A healer."

"She's a folk doctor?"

Gabriel crossed the room and sat down beside her. She smelled of soap, clean and enticing. He stretched his legs out in front of him, cupping the glass in his palms. Out on the lake a boat cruised by, its bright deck lights appearing like fallen stars on the smooth black of the water.

"It's like a folk doctor, although a *traiteur* is a specialist—he or she can only treat one thing. And unlike traditional folk medicine, the patient doesn't have to believe in the powers of the healer. Only the healer needs to believe."

"What's your grandmother's specialty?"

"Headaches. There probably isn't a headache that cranky old woman can't cure."

"Too bad she doesn't make house calls," Eve murmured. "I think I could use a miracle cure."

Gabriel studied her thoughtfully. Then he placed his glass on the marble table in front of them.

Eve was unnerved by the sudden gleam in his dark eyes. "What are you doing?"

"Relax," he said soothingly as he plucked the mug out of her hands and put it beside his glass.

"Gabriel—"

"Shhh. Just relax."

Relax? How did he expect her to relax when his dark chocolate eyes were observing her with such warmth? And his body was leaning so very, very close to hers.

"Really," she protested, "I don't think—"

"That's right," he crooned. "Don't think. Not now. Just close your eyes and go with the flow." His thumbs began to make slow, steady circles on her temples.

Eve wanted to protest. She wanted to insist that it was time for him to go home. She knew she should object, tell him he had no right to be touching her like this. But, dear God, his gentle caresses felt so very, very good.

"That's it," he murmured approvingly as he watched her eyelids flutter shut. "Now imagine waves of light. Waves of warm, golden light, shimmering through you . . . soft, glowing light, flowing throughout your body. Velvety light, soothing light."

Eve felt as if she was drifting on gentle waves as her body responded to Gabriel's soft commands. Warmth seemed to leave his fingertips and enter her bloodstream, flowing through her, down her legs, through her arms, to her fingertips, in waves of golden, shimmering light. Her mind cleared. There was only now. Only this warm, glowing moment.

The color was back in her cheeks, blooming under the honey of her tan like late summer roses. Her lips were slightly parted, her breath, as it slipped between them, was scented with fresh mint. Gabriel reminded himself that he only wanted to comfort her, to soothe her pain. But then his body stirred insistently in response to the provocative picture she made, causing a slow ache deep in his loins, and all his good intentions went flying right out those spotless, floor-to-ceiling windows.

"Eve."

She was floating on gentle swells of sunlit waters. She couldn't recall ever feeling so relaxed. "Mmmm?"

"Open your eyes."

His hands were warm and strong and gentle as they cradled her head. Eve luxuriated in the feeling. Her eyelids felt heavy; to lift them would be an effort she didn't feel quite up to.

"Why?"

"Because I'm going to kiss you," he said patiently. "And I'd like your full attention when I do."

5

HIS WORDS HAD the desired effect. Eve's eyelids flew open, and she found herself staring right into Gabriel's hypnotic eyes. She swallowed.

"I don't think that would be a very good idea."

His long fingers were cupping her jaw; his thumb traced her lower lip. There was a hint of humor in his eyes as he raised a dark brow.

"Don't tell me you're afraid of a simple kiss."

Eve had already determined that there was nothing simple about Gabriel. He was at once the most intriguing and most annoying man she'd ever met. "Of course not," she said in her mildest voice. But she looked at him with obvious mistrust.

"I didn't think that was the case. Not after you've already demonstrated an amazing wealth of courage this evening."

She might be brave—to a point, that is—but she wasn't stupid. "Gabriel, I honestly don't believe this is a very good idea."

"You're probably right. But at the moment I'm having a helluva time thinking of a better one. How about you?"

"No." Her soft, breathless voice was a whisper of surrender. "I can't."

Gabriel's answering sigh could have been one of satisfaction or relief, Eve couldn't be quite sure. She was still attempting to decide when he lowered his head. Without a word their mouths met in slow, mutual pleasure. It was not at all what she had anticipated. There was gentleness where she'd been expecting insistence, patience rather than power. It was, in a word, beguiling. The breath Eve had been unaware of holding shuddered out in a long, trembling sigh in the second before Gabriel's lips fused to hers.

Desire swirled up, stunning her with its intensity; when his tongue traced a ring of exquisite fire around the perimeter of her parted lips, she felt as if she'd been hurled headlong into a hurricane. As she moved her hands up to rest on his shoulders—strong shoulders, she noted dazedly—Eve decided that thinking could come later.

Gabriel felt her resistance ebb. He felt it in the softening of her lips, the strength of her fingers as they clutched his shoulders. Heat simmered at the base of his spine, making him ache. Still he refused to rush. He forced himself to continue kissing her slowly, lingeringly, even as he proceeded to drive himself insane.

The kiss was like a seductive whisper against her mouth, soft as thistledown and tasting of cognac. Cognac and carefully restrained passion. It was only a kiss, Eve reminded herself as his tongue traced a damp, silky pattern across her trembling lips. A mere merging of lips. Nothing more. But oh, how it was making **her blood hum!**

When he slipped his tongue between her lips, her breath caught. She released it in a soft, ragged moan that burned away the last of his tautly held restraint. His tongue breached the silken barrier of her lips, invading her, possessing her in a way that was agonizingly erotic. Eve clung to him, reveling in the taste of his mouth, the hard, masculine pressure of his body as he lowered her onto the white sofa.

Pressure from his body. . . and something else. Reality abruptly intruded as she felt the cold, hard steel of the revolver against her hip.

"No."

It was only a whisper, but Gabriel heard it easily in the stillness of the room. Reminding himself that this was a woman who prided herself on her intellect and self-restraint, Gabriel slowly drew away.

"That shouldn't have happened," Eve insisted quietly.

Gabriel didn't answer immediately. Instead, leaving the sofa, he retrieved his glass of cognac from the marble table and walked over to the terrace door, where he stood gazing out over the moonlit lake. Eve, who had been expecting sputtered protests, watched him warily from the corner of the sofa.

After what seemed an eternity, he turned around, fixing her with a steady, sober gaze. "You're right."

It was not at all what she'd expected him to say. "I am?"

"You sound surprised that I agree with you."

Suspecting a trap, Eve warned herself to remain unmoved by the intimate warmth in Gabriel's smile. "I am."

He threw back his head and finished off the cognac. When he met her wary eyes once again, his own gaze turned somewhat apologetic.

"Look, Eve, you're a nice woman. Not to mention being a remarkably intelligent one. And beautiful, to boot." He grinned encouragingly. "Actually, if you were a baseball player, I suppose you could be viewed as a triple threat."

"Thanks," she murmured. "I think."

"It was meant as a compliment," he assured her. "The thing is, sweetheart, that fear—not to mention danger—is a proven aphrodisiac."

"Which explains what happened between us," Eve said.

He nodded. "Exactly. Believe me, take one reasonably attractive male and one drop-dead-gorgeous female, toss in some danger, shake vigorously, and you'll end up with what just happened on that pristine white couch of yours."

She felt a slight stirring of doubt and ignored it. What Gabriel was saying was logical. And practical. And Eve was a logical, practical individual.

"I suppose that could be a reasonable explanation," she agreed thoughtfully.

Gabriel's expression was one of immense satisfaction. "That's exactly what happened," he assured her as he put his glass back down on the trolley and headed toward the door. "So there's no point in beating ourselves to death over it. What's done is done. We'll simply go on from here." As he heard the words coming out of his mouth, Gabriel grimaced, wondering if there was a cliché he had failed to dredge up.

Eve rose from the couch to accompany him. "Thank you," she said politely. "I feel much better about things now."

"I'm glad. No offense, Eve, but as beautiful as you are, you really aren't my type."

"Then we're even," she agreed conversationally, wondering why his words stung and deciding it was nothing more than understandable female pride. "Because you're not my type, either."

He paused in the doorway and looked down at her. "I'm glad we got that settled."

"Especially since we're going to be working together," she agreed.

Her calm eyes seemed incredibly deep. Gabriel felt as if he could drown in their vivid blue depths. "I take it that means you're going to continue to tag along on this investigation?"

Tag along? Anger rose to stamp out over any passion that might be lingering deep within her. "Not during the day." She forced her voice to remain cool. She wouldn't give him the satisfaction of making her lose her temper. "After all, I do have my work—"

"Ah, yes, I should have known you'd never be one to shirk your duty."

She glanced at him sharply, thinking she detected a hint of mockery in his tone. His expression gave nothing away. "My work is important."

"Did I say it wasn't?"

"It wasn't what you said. It was more what you implied."

As intriguing sparks flashed once again in her eyes, Gabriel wondered if his careful, albeit clichéd words of explanation had been meant to convince Eve that there was nothing between them—or to convince himself. He took hold of her hand, brushing his thumb over her knuckles. When he felt her slight tremor, Gabriel was forced to acknowledge that yet another complication had just been added to what had appeared to be a routine missing person case.

"Let's not waste time arguing," he suggested. "We've had a rough night, and both of us are facing a hectic day tomorrow. Oh, that reminds me. Joe Reardon is going to want to question you."

Her hand went cold in his. "He wants to question me? About what?"

Gabriel squeezed her fingers. "It's just routine."

"Will I have to go down to the police station?"

"No. He's agreed to keep you out of this as much as possible—he'll come by your office."

"Would you think me silly if I told you that I hate the idea of talking with a policeman?"

"A lot of people feel that way. It's only normal. But you don't have to worry in this case. Joe and I were partners for a long time, and believe me, he's one of the good guys."

She managed to return his smile with a faint one of her own. "Is he as good as you?"

Gabriel laughed. The deep, rich sound sent a wave of reassuring warmth flowing through her. "Hell, sweetheart, no one's as good as me."

Unable to resist, he ducked his head and kissed her swiftly on the lips. "Lock this door," he instructed. "And don't forget to put on the security chain."

Her lips were still tingling from the unexpected contact. "Really, Gabriel," she complained at his somewhat overbearing tone, "I'm quite capable of taking care of myself."

He caught her chin between his fingers and gave her a long, warning look. "We're not playing with amateurs here, Eve. I don't want anything to happen to you."

Her mouth went instantly dry; she resisted the urge to lick her lips. "That makes two of us."

He smiled at her weak attempt at humor. "Lock the door," he repeated. And then he was gone.

LATER THAT NIGHT Gabriel's fingers were laced together behind his head as he lay on his back in bed, fantasizing about Eve dressed in a lace-edged, white satin teddy. The brief teddy displayed her slender but decidedly appealing curves to advantage and made her legs look as though they went on forever. Her blue eyes were sparkling with a remarkably sensual combination of desire and demureness. His body stirred pleasantly.

Lying in the darkness, Gabriel assured himself that his feelings of sexual arousal were not actually stimulated by Eve but by the fact that it had been a very long time since he'd been with a woman. Probably too long. But establishing his own agency had taken the bulk of his energies over the past few years and hadn't given him the time to establish a worthwhile relationship with a woman. And although Gabriel knew he could be considered something of an anachronism, he had never been into recreational sex, even during the heyday of the sexual revolution.

What he needed, he realized now, was to allocate more time to his personal life. Perhaps once this Harry Keegan business was over with, he'd begin looking for a woman capable of piquing his interest.

There was, of course, a woman who'd already done just that, Gabriel admitted, as he fantasized slipping the straps of the teddy off her shoulders, one at a time, permitting his lips access to her creamy shoulders. The gleaming satin clung tenuously to her breasts; the slightest tug would send it slipping to the lush white carpet underfoot.

The thought of Eve's nude body, illuminated by warm, flickering candlelight, caused Gabriel's vague sexual stirring to escalate into a throbbing ache that had him cursing under his breath. By the time the day dawned bright and sunny, he was forced to admit that the feelings he'd been experiencing with alarming regularity over the past two days had not been brought about by his need for a warm female body in his bed, but by his growing desire for one particular woman. Eve.

GABRIEL WAS NOT THE ONLY ONE to experience a restless night. Across town, for the second night in a row, Eve tossed and turned, mental images of Harry Keegan, Dixie, Gabriel Bouvier and that man—always that dead man—tumbling around in her head like the facets of a child's kaleidoscope. Constantly changing, whirling, shifting, but never leaving her at peace.

Finally, shortly before dawn, she surrendered. Getting up from her rumpled bed, she went to the kitchen and made a cup of instant coffee. Then she went out onto the terrace to watch the sun rise.

The early-morning air was already warm and muggy, forecasting another day of record temperatures. She'd read in yesterday's paper that crime rose during heat waves. As she sipped her coffee, she wondered if the man in Harry's apartment had simply been one of those unsavory statistics. Perhaps he had been a burglar, caught in the act of committing a crime. Perhaps he had nothing at all to do with Harry. And therefore nothing to do with her.

But if he'd been a burglar, then Harry would have been the logical one to have caught him burglarizing the apartment. If that were the case, it would follow that Harry was the one who'd shot him. Once again Harry was at the center of the puzzle. So what else was new?

She propped her bare feet on the low concrete wall of the terrace. The sun was coming over the horizon, splintering the clouds with streaks of pink and lavender. Perhaps today she would have some answers to the riddle that was Harry Keegan. Perhaps Gabriel would discover the key.

Gabriel. Eve sighed. He was like no one she'd ever met. He was strong, utterly masculine, yet sensitive enough to know when to be tender. A man who, although he'd undoubtedly witnessed unspeakable violence, could speak easily and lovingly of his family. Gabriel Bouvier knew how to laugh—indeed, for a time she'd wondered if he took anything seriously—but from the way his expression had sobered when he'd talked about the futility of death, Eve had the feeling he was also a man who knew how to cry.

As for the kisses they'd shared... Eve had spent a good portion of her sleepless night trying to recall the last time she'd been kissed like that and had finally come to the reluctant conclusion that she had *never* been kissed like that. If it hadn't been for his gun... She shook her head, embarrassed even now that she'd experienced a passion powerful enough to cause her to shed her self-control, which had been a lifetime in the making.

Eve couldn't deny that she'd been attracted to him. What woman wouldn't be? The man was gorgeous, in a lean, rugged, Clint Eastwood sort of way. Sexy. He was also trouble with a capital T. Trouble she had every intention of avoiding.

The rising sun had painted the waters of the lake a sleek and gleaming gold. Finishing her coffee, Eve rose from her chair with renewed determination that from now on, her relationship with Gabriel Bouvier would remain strictly business.

HARRY KEEGAN'S APARTMENT had been cordoned off with yellow police tape. Gabriel, intent on examining the room himself, was engaged in a heated argument with the uniformed patrolman at the door when Joe Reardon suddenly showed up.

"You know the rules, Gabriel," Reardon said. "You want first dibs on the crime scene, rejoin the force. Not that it'd do you much good—except for a spent slug, the place is clean. If Keegan was actually living there, he was the world's best housekeeper. No personal effects, no hairs, no prints—"

"I told you he was a phantom," Gabriel reminded his former partner.

"Right. So I suppose that makes us Ghostbusters, right?" He scowled as he lit a cigarette. "What're you doing here so early? Don't you ever sleep?"

Gabriel shrugged. "Speaking of sleeping, what are you doing working double shifts? I figured by the time a guy made detective first grade, he could coast."

"You figured wrong," Reardon said. "I've been assigned to head up the task force."

The apartment door was open, as was the door to the bathroom. The body had been removed, but a chalk outline had been drawn on the green linoleum. Inside the chalk was a dark stain in the shape of a giant amoeba.

"A task force?" Gabriel asked. "Since when does the department get overly upset over some guy getting gunned down in a flophouse?"

"Since the guy is a fed."

Gabriel's eyes narrowed. "A fed? As in FBI?"

Reardon nodded. "Got it on the first try. So you want to tell me what you and Ms Eve Whitfield have in common with a dead FBI agent?"

"Not a thing?"

The detective didn't bother to conceal his irritation. "Dammit, Gabriel, I've got brass climbing all over me on this one. So why don't you be a good guy and tell me what you know? Or do I have to drag you and the illustrious CEO of Whitfield Palace Hotels down to the station?"

"Next thing I know, you'll be threatening me with the rubber hoses."

"Look, I've had a long night, and as soon as the press finds out exactly who we've got here, this thing is going to turn into a three-ring circus. I'm not in the mood for any of your smart-ass remarks this morning."

"Better watch it, Joe. Your blood pressure looks like it's going to go off the chart. Have you thought about taking up running? It'd do you a world of good." Gabriel patted his flat stomach. "Keeps you fit. And relaxed. Something that wouldn't hurt you in the least, by the way."

"Relax? You want to tell me how I'm going to relax when I've got one floater with half of Lake Pontchartrain in his lungs, another who's been shot with the first guy's gun—"

"Wait a minute." Gabriel held up his hand. "Are you talking about Mad Max?"

Reardon's look was one of simmering frustration. "Of course I am. I told you about finding him in the lake two days ago."

"So you did," Gabriel agreed thoughtfully. "And you think he's the one who killed the guy in the apartment?"

"I don't think so, I know so. The guys spent yesterday dragging the lake and came up with a .44 Super Blackhawk."

"Max's weapon of choice."

"Exactly. Then we found a slug in the bathroom wall last night."

"A .44?"

"Hey, you must be getting smarter in your old age. So anyway, I talked Kolb down in ballistics into doing a rush job on the slug and—"

"I've never known Pete Kolb to rush anything. Unless it's closing down the lab early so he can make it to Dooley's in time for happy hour."

"He owed me fifty bucks from last week's poker game. I called him at home around midnight and promised to write it off if he'd get me a preliminary report by this morning."

"And?"

Reardon took a long drag on his cigarette. "And the slug that went through our victim and ended up in the bathroom wall came from Mad Max's gun."

Gabriel whistled under his breath. "That's a pretty heavy hit. Even for Max. Think he knew the guy was FBI?"

"Why wouldn't he?"

Gabriel weighed his obligation to keep the case confidential against Eve's safety and opted for keeping her alive. Besides, he figured, it wasn't as if he were a priest or a doctor or anything like that. "Because of this." He reached into his pocket, extracting a photocopy of the newspaper clipping. "Does he look familiar?"

"Yeah," Reardon said without hesitation, "it's the guy from the floor. The fed."

"That's exactly what I first thought last night. But it's not him, Joe. This picture is of Harry Keegan."

Joe Reardon rubbed his unshaven chin. His eyes under heavily hooded lids were skeptical. "You sure?"

"Positive."

"The phantom," Reardon muttered.

"None other. A phantom who bears a striking resemblance to the dead man in Keegan's apartment. If a pair of brilliant detectives like you and I could confuse the two of them, why couldn't Max?"

"You've got a point," Reardon said. "As farfetched as it may be. What's your connection with Keegan?"

"He seems to be missing. I'm looking for him."

"For Eve Whitfield?"

"Could be."

"What does a woman with all she's got going for her want with a two-bit crook suddenly turned murder suspect?"

Gabriel shook his head. "It's a family matter, Joe. It doesn't have anything to do with this."

Reardon didn't bother to hide his skepticism. "If you're hiding anything that could help with this case, Gabe, so help me God, I'll break both your arms."

"I wouldn't expect anything else. Meanwhile, while my arms are still intact, why don't I get a handball court for later this afternoon?"

"This sudden desire for a handball partner is just your way to pump me about whatever else we come up with today, isn't it?"

"I can't deny that had crossed my mind," Gabriel said with a quick grin. "Although I prefer to think of it as sharing information. After all, I'm working this case, too, albeit from a different angle. And I am the best private investigator in town."

"Says who?"

"Richard Owens."

"*The* Richard Owens? Of Owens and Martin? The renowned private security firm preferred by the cream of the *Fortune* 500? The agency with branches in Paris, London and Rome?"

"You forgot Rio de Janeiro. And yes, it's the same Richard Owens who hands over all his really tough cases to yours truly."

"Pretty lofty company you're running around with these days. Have you considered buying a new suit so you don't look like the janitor when you're hanging around all those executive office buildings in the CBD?"

"There you go again, casting aspersions on my attire, when we both know you're just jealous of my dashing good looks," Gabriel complained good-naturedly. "I'll get the court for four o'clock. It'll do you good."

"Just let me know if you find this Keegan guy. God, I hate mysteries," the detective muttered as he returned to the room.

RATHER THAN SEND SOMEONE from the company to retrieve her car, Eve took a taxi to Audubon Place. She found her mother in the solarium, wearing a satin dressing gown covered with brilliant tropical flowers. She was reading the current issue of *Town and Country* magazine; a stack of opened mail was beside her breakfast plate.

Dixie looked up from the glossy magazine and smiled. "Good morning, darling. What a nice surprise."

Eve bent to kiss her cheek. Her fragrance echoed the vivid flowers on her gown. "I came to pick up my car."

"I wasn't surprised that you'd left with Gabriel last night," Dixie said serenely as she poured a second cup of coffee from the sterling-silver pot and handed it to Eve. "Not the way the sparks were flying between the two of you."

"There weren't any sparks between Gabriel Bouvier and me."

Dixie chuckled. "Of course there were, dear." She selected a plump blueberry muffin from a plate of freshly baked pastries. "And you certainly don't have to apologize for being attracted to the man, darling. Any woman would be. That vague, underlying sense of danger surrounding him is quite appealing." She blushed prettily. "There's something highly irresistible about a man of mystery."

"Speaking of mystery men . . ."

"You still don't approve of my decision to marry Harry, do you?"

Eve looked down at the table. No words were necessary; her guilty look told it all.

"I love him, darling," Dixie insisted softly. "More than I ever thought possible. Did you and Gabriel learn anything about Harry's disappearance last night?"

Eve thought of the man lying on Harry Keegan's bathroom floor, his eyes staring sightlessly at the ceiling. "No," she lied, wanting to spare her mother the unpleasant knowledge that the felonious Keegan had possibly added murder to his list of crimes. "Nothing at all."

"I'm certain Gabriel will find him soon."

"That's right," Eve said dryly. "How could I forget? Madame Leblanc's chicken bones are never wrong."

"Madame Leblanc only confirmed what I already knew," Dixie countered firmly. "Knew deep in here." She pressed her palm over her heart.

Eve's own heart went out to her mother even as her worry escalated to new heights. In the beginning it had all seemed so simple: find Harry Keegan, pay him off, then stand by to dry her mother's tears when her thief-lover failed to return. But now that Harry was mixed up in murder, it was going to be more difficult to keep Dixie from learning about his unsavory past.

Try as she might, Eve couldn't think of any way to shield her mother from a great deal of emotional pain. Douglas Whitfield had treated his wife like a delicate, hothouse orchid, something to be appreciated and cared for. When he had died, the mantle of responsibility had fallen on Eve's shoulders. She only hoped she could live up to her promise to watch out for Dixie. To keep her safe.

"I hope you're right, Mama," she said softly.

Dixie looked momentarily surprised at Eve's use of a word she'd declared too childish in the fifth grade. "Don't you worry about all this, darling," she said, patting her daughter's hand reassuringly, "everything is going to turn out wonderfully. You'll see—I have a sixth sense about such things." She smiled blissfully. "Perhaps we should have the wedding right here in the garden. Wouldn't that be nice?"

"Lovely," Eve said softly. There was no point in arguing. Not when cruel reality would be shattering Dixie's idyllic little dreamworld soon enough.

6

THE PREVIOUS NIGHT'S RAIN had been a short-lived fluke
of nature. Instead of cooling the city down, all it had
done was raise the humidity another ten points. By
three o'clock the streets were baking, and Gabriel Bouvier was sweating. Fortunately, the executive offices of
Whitfield Towers were air-conditioned, providing a
welcome sanctuary from the stifling heat.

The reception area was chic and expensively decorated: silver-gray carpeting, molded lacquered furniture, contemporary art prints in slim aluminum frames
on the walls. The face of the beautiful redhead busily
typing away on a gray word processor behind the desk
could have graced the cover of any fashion magazine.

"May I help you?" she asked, frowning as she cast a
second glance at his rumpled clothing.

"I'm here to see Ms Whitfield."

"Of course, sir. If I may just have your name . . ."

"Gabriel Bouvier."

"Bouvier?"

"That's right. B-o-u-v-i-e-r. Bouvier."

The receptionist ran a carmine-painted nail down the
edge of her appointment calendar, a puzzled expression on her face. "Do you have an appointment, Mr.
Bouvier?"

"No, but—"

She shook her titian head, giving him a regretful smile he suspected was every bit as phony as her hair color. "I'm sorry, but Ms Whitfield has a very busy day scheduled. If you'd like to make an appointment, I can pencil you in on..." She flipped through the book. "August twentieth." Her smile widened, revealing dazzling white teeth.

"I'd prefer to see her now."

"But—"

He leaned over the desk and picked up the receiver of the gray telephone. "Why don't you buzz Ms Whitfield and tell her I'm here," he suggested quietly.

"Really, sir—"

"Please."

The young woman looked at the determination on his face. After a moment, she took the receiver he was holding toward her, reached for one of the Lucite buttons, hesitated, then pressed it.

"Ms Whitfield," she said hurriedly, apologetically, "I hate to bother you, but there's a gentleman out here—" She paused. "His name is Mr. Bouvier. B-o-u—"

Then she stopped talking in order to listen to the voice on the other end of the intercom line. "Yes, Ms Whitfield. Of course. I'll tell him."

As she replaced the receiver in the cradle, the receptionist eyed Gabriel with renewed interest, giving him the distinct impression that not many people entered Eve Whitfield's inner sanctum without having made an appointment at least six weeks in advance.

"Ms Whitfield says that if you'll take a seat, she'll be right with you. She's on the telephone at the moment. Long-distance," she added significantly.

Gabriel sat down on a gray-and-white silk-covered chair, picked up a copy of *Architectural Digest* from a nearby table and prepared to wait. A moment later the intercom buzzed.

"Yes, Ms Whitfield," the receptionist responded briskly. "Yes, I'll send him right in."

She looked over at Gabriel, giving him a bright, professional smile that belied their earlier battle of wills. "Ms Whitfield will see you now."

As Eve stood up from behind the black lacquered desk to greet him, she was the personification of a bright April morning: sunny hair, eyes like cornflowers, a wheat-colored suit and a silk blouse the color of jonquils.

"Hello," she said in that intriguing husky voice he hadn't been able to get out of his mind the past two nights. "I'm sorry to have kept you waiting." She smiled, and sunshine filled the room.

"No problem." Gabriel remained standing in the doorway, perfectly content to enjoy the scenery.

"Are you going to come in and sit down, or are we going to have to use signal flags to communicate across the room?"

"It *is* a rather large office," he said, walking across the expanse of thick silver pile to a chair on the visitor's side of the desk.

"Much larger than I need. But my father always felt that first impressions are extremely important."

"How do you feel?" Gabriel was relieved when the sleek, molded aluminum and gray suede chair proved to be more comfortable than it appeared at first glance.

She shrugged as she reclaimed her own high-backed seat, which was upholstered in a smooth, glove-soft gray leather. "Why, I agree with him, of course."

"Of course," Gabriel murmured, wondering why he'd even bothered asking the question. It appeared that in the eyes of his daughter, Douglas Whitfield could do no wrong.

"You don't like it."

He glanced around the office, which was every bit as chic as the reception area. And every bit as sterile as Eve's lakeshore condominium. Since it was obvious that a great deal of money had gone into the hard-edged decor, he decided it would be prudent to keep his uncomplimentary thoughts to himself.

"Sure I do."

"I distinctly heard implied criticism in your tone."

He got up, walked around the desk and perched on the corner. Unable to resist, he smoothed the small lines that had appeared between her blond brows. "Didn't your mama ever warn you that if you keep frowning like that, you're going to get wrinkles?"

Eve forced herself to hold her ground as she glared at him. "Really—"

"Your skin is so remarkably soft," he murmured, ignoring her protest. "I spent most of last night trying to think of what it reminded me of."

His eyes remained steadfastly on hers as his finger trailed slowly, intimately, down her cheek. "The closest thing I could come up with was the underside of rose petals. Or gardenias." The gentle caress continued along the firm line of her jaw. "But even they didn't quite measure up."

The brush of his fingertips felt like a mild breeze fluttering against her skin. No one had ever affected her so deeply with such a seemingly innocent touch.

Too fast. Once again it was all happening too fast. Eve pulled away. "I believe we were discussing my office."

The cool, remote look in her eyes didn't fool him in the least. Something had passed between them, something dark and potent. Something they would both have to deal with later.

Gabriel returned to his chair, leaned back and linked his fingers behind his head. "No," he corrected reflectively, "we were discussing whether or not I like your office, although I can't figure out why you should give a damn what I think."

Neither could Eve. That was precisely what had her feeling so out of sorts. "I've never been particularly good at obligatory small talk," she said, folding her hands on the desk. "So why don't we just get down to your reason for being here?"

Gabriel wondered whether she was aware of giving out such mixed signals. One minute she was the brisk, no-nonsense head of a multinational corporation. Then, without a blink of her wide blue eyes, she could make him want to get up, lock the office door and find out exactly what feminine secrets she was hiding under that severely tailored linen suit.

"I came to invite you to dinner."

"That's all?"

"That's about it."

"What about Harry?"

"I'm working on it."

"What about the dead FBI agent? By the way, I want to thank you for calling and warning me about that before my interview with Detective Reardon."

"I figured you were nervous enough about meeting with Joe. I didn't want to leave him to break the news. How did you two get along?"

"Very well. You were right."

"Of course. After you get to know me better, you'll come to learn that I'm always right. What was I right about this time?"

"Detective Reardon is a very nice man. Needless to say, I was horribly nervous, but he has this funny way about him—I can't quite describe it—that put me right at ease."

Gabriel smiled as he recalled his former partner's uncanny ability to be liked by everyone. "He promised me he'd lay off the third degree. For old time's sake."

"I'm afraid I wasn't very helpful in his investigation."

"Don't worry about it. Neither was I. I like that blouse," he said, abruptly changing the subject. "It reminds me of springtime." His dark eyes swept over her in a slow, appreciative study. "Actually, the rest of you reminds me of spring, too. April. In Paris. Have you ever been to Paris, Eve?"

"Of course. We have a hotel there; I used to do the surprise inspections."

"You went to Paris to work?"

"Of course. About Harry Keegan—"

"In the spring?"

"I suppose I've been there in the spring. I can't recall the exact dates. Now about that car last night—"

"But you took time to mix a little pleasure with your business, right?" he asked hopefully.

"Actually, whenever I go abroad, my itinerary is quite full. We have a great many interests in Europe and I prefer not to waste valuable time. Could we please just get back to—"

"That's terrible. No one goes to Paris in the spring to work."

"I do. Now—"

"What a waste." He shook his head.

"You're entitled to your opinion, I suppose. Returning to Harry—"

Gabriel glanced down at his watch. "As much as I've enjoyed this little chat, I have to be going—I'm playing handball in twenty minutes."

"Handball?"

"That's right."

"Am I to understand that I'm paying you five hundred dollars a day—"

"Plus expenses," he said helpfully.

"—five hundred dollars per day, plus expenses, to play handball?"

"Not exactly. You are paying five hundred dollars a day, plus expenses, for me to spend the morning and most of the afternoon—which resulted in my missing lunch entirely, by the way—trying to run down some of Harry Keegan's shady associates. You are also paying five hundred dollars per day, plus expenses, for me to play handball with the head of the task force investigating the murder of one FBI agent found dead in the aforementioned Harry Keegan's apartment. Where, in the privacy of a closed court, Detective Reardon and I will have an opportunity to compare notes, thus cut-

ting my investigation time—and ultimately your
costs—in half." He gave her a long, challenging look.
"Does that answer your question, Ms Whitfield?"

There was something new in his voice. A cold, precise anger that came as a surprise. "I'm sorry," she
murmured. "I'm afraid I jumped to the wrong conclusion."

"Next time perhaps you should look before you
leap," Gabriel suggested. Although his tone was de-
ceptively mild, Eve knew she'd been warned.

"Perhaps I should."

The carefully restrained temper disappeared from his
eyes as he gave her a slow, unsettling smile. "Now that
we've got that straight, how about dinner?"

"I don't think that would be a very good idea," she
murmured, fiddling with a crystal paperweight.

Gabriel eyed her thoughtfully. "You're worried about
a repeat performance of last night," he said with the
uncanny perceptiveness she was beginning to expect
from him.

"Yes." She met his smiling eyes with a level look of her
own. "Things became far too personal last night. I've
never been very good at playing games. Especially sexual ones."

"Is that what you think I've been doing? Playing
sexual games with you?"

"Isn't it?"

"Not at all." He leaned forward, his elbows on his
knees, his fingers linked between his legs. "Look, Eve,
the only reason I suggested dinner is that we should get
together and discuss your case. Since I missed lunch,
I'll be starving by evening, and even a brilliant detective like me tends to think much better on a full stom-

ach. Believe me, not only do real private investigators not drive around in fancy sports cars, we don't automatically tumble into bed with all our female clients, either. Even the beautiful ones." He smiled at her. "Does that ease your mind?"

Eve felt the telltale color rising in her cheeks and couldn't do anything to prevent it. "Yes, I believe it does."

"Good. How about seven-thirty? That'll give you time to go home and change."

"Change?" She glanced down at her suit.

"I thought that given the heat, you'd like to slip into something more comfortable."

Alarm bells sounded in her head. "Where exactly are we having this business dinner?"

"I thought I'd throw something together at my place. Why?"

Eve was about to answer with a million reasons why she would not be having an intimate dinner for two at Gabriel Bouvier's home, when the intercom buzzed.

"Yes?" she snapped uncharacteristically. "What is it?"

"They're ready for you in the eighth-floor conference room, Ms Whitfield. Shall I relay the message that you've been detained?"

Eve realized that her secretary's timely interruption had saved her from making a tactical error. If she allowed this man to know how easily he had unnerved her, she'd lose what little control she still maintained over the situation.

"I'll be right down. A home-cooked meal sounds lovely," she said, returning her attention to Gabriel.

Gabriel's grin was quick and appealing. "Prepare yourself for the best meal you've ever had."

Eve couldn't resist a slight smile of her own. "You certainly don't have a self-confidence problem, do you?"

"Me?" He opened his eyes wide and put his hand against his chest. "Why, I'm the most modest and bashful man you'd ever want to meet."

"Really."

He nodded as he rose from the chair. "Sure I am. Just like all Cajuns."

Eve laughed at that outrageous understatement. "I'll see you at seven-thirty," she agreed, walking with him to the door. "What's the address?" She wasn't surprised when he gave her a street number in the Quarter. "Can I bring something?"

They were standing in the open doorway to her office, in full view of the avidly interested receptionist. "That's not necessary," Gabriel said. Then he changed his mind. "I take that back. There is something I'd appreciate your bringing."

"Wine?"

"Uh-uh. A smile."

She stared up at him. "A what?"

"A smile." Before Eve could guess his intent, Gabriel had cupped her chin in his hand. "You have the loveliest smile, *chérie*," he murmured, tracing the outline of her lips with his thumbnail. "You should use it more often."

He lowered his head and pressed his mouth against hers. The brief kiss was over as soon as it had begun, but that didn't stop her head from spinning. Gabriel, she noticed with irritation, appeared remarkably unmoved.

"I'll see you this evening. Come hungry."

As he walked past the desk, he tipped an imaginary hat to the receptionist, who appeared every bit as startled as Eve by what had just taken place. Both women watched Gabriel amble out of the office, hands in the back pockets of his faded jeans. He was whistling.

7

A SLIDE PRESENTATION took up the latter part of the meeting with the hotel executives, and as Eve sat in the dark, trying to keep her mind on the newest hotel in the chain, her thoughts drifted back to Gabriel. There was nothing in the brief conversation she could fault him for. He'd been friendly, polite, reasonable.

Oh, he'd touched her, but that in itself was no crime. Eve had come to the conclusion a long time ago that the world was divided into two groups of people—the touchers and the non-touchers. Her mother, for instance, seemed unable to keep her slender hands to herself. Like graceful birds, they continually fluttered, caressingly, reassuringly. It was not any attempt to invade personal space; it was simply Dixie's way. During their short acquaintance Eve had come to realize that Gabriel was also a toucher.

Eve was not.

The simple act of smoothing away a few frown lines couldn't be viewed as a prelude to sexual assault. Although she had no proof, she suspected he would have behaved just the same way with his mother or a child. If events were viewed rationally, it could be argued that Gabriel hadn't intended any intimate connotations with the gesture.

But if that were honestly the case, then why had he compared her skin to rose petals? Or gardenias? Even now she could feel her cheeks warm at the memory of his tender touch, his lush, velvety dark voice. And that brief but fiery kiss . . . There was a low murmur of disapproval. Eve blinked, forcing her attention back to a slide of the fountain adorning the lobby of the Kathmandu Whitfield Palace.

All the Whitfield hotels were called palaces; it had been her father's rule that guests deserved to be treated like royalty. But she admitted that some locations lived up to the creed better than others. The Kathmandu Whitfield Palace, open only six months, was turning out to be one of the less spectacular examples of American hospitality.

Eve made a note on the legal pad beside her to instruct someone to teach the maintenance people about the benefits of chlorine. The water in the fountain was a dark forest green; a layer of algae bobbed on the bubbling surface. As the scene changed to the exquisitely appointed gold-domed dining room, Eve's thoughts wandered once again.

Eve's entire life had centered around Whitfield Palace Hotels from the time she began accompanying her father to the office when she was five. By age seven she had visited all fifteen Whitfield Palaces. As her father continued to build more and more hotels, Eve continued attending the opening ceremonies, first as a guest, later as part of the management team.

All her life she'd worked hard to become a woman her father could be proud of—a woman capable of controlling a worldwide enterprise. Eve had learned that weak men didn't survive very long in the jungle that men like Douglas Whitfield had created. Soft women . . . well, a soft woman would get eaten alive.

Before breakfast. So she'd built tough emotional defenses that she wore like a second skin, and they'd always served her well. Until now. Until Gabriel Bouvier. Every instinct Eve possessed told her that this was a man who could rip away those defenses and leave her exposed. Vulnerable. Something she could not, under any circumstances, permit to happen.

The problem was, Eve considered glumly, how did she go about preventing the inevitable?

She was struggling with that question when a puzzled voice filtered through her preoccupation. Looking up, she was startled to find that the lights had been turned on again. The men seated around the mahogany table were wearing identical navy suits, white shirts and yellow ties, which she'd read somewhere was the new power color. They were also all staring at her.

"Eve—" Blake Carstairs, her executive assistant, repeated her name "—what do you think?"

What on earth had he asked her? Eve took a shot in the dark. "I think the photo presentation was very well done," she ad-libbed. "Although I do have some suggestions—"

"We were talking about having dinner sent in."

"Dinner?"

"Well, I assumed you'd want to keep working, and it is getting late."

Eve glanced down at her watch. Seven-fifteen. So much for going home and changing her clothes. She'd be lucky to make it to the French Quarter on time.

"You're right," she agreed, abruptly pushing her chair back from the table. "Why don't we adjourn this meeting until tomorrow morning?"

The face of everyone in the room registered polite surprise. Blake, who had worked with her the longest, was less discreet. He was openly staring at her. "Adjourn?"

"It's been a long, frustrating day. I think we could all use an evening to relax before tackling the problem tomorrow." Her cool gaze swept the table. "Are there any objections?"

Dark heads, all with the same carefully styled haircut, shook in unison.

"Fine," she said. "Then we'll meet tomorrow morning at nine o'clock sharp. Good night, gentlemen."

As the men scrambled to their feet, the surprise on their faces changed to relief, which in turn changed to anticipation. They resembled a group of schoolboys who'd just been let out of class early.

As Eve walked out of the office, she found herself feeling exactly the same way.

THE RED MESSAGE LIGHT on his telephone recorder was blinking when Gabriel entered the apartment. Getting himself a beer from the refrigerator, he plopped down on the sofa, put his feet up on the coffee table and began listening to the messages.

Beep. "Hi, Gabriel. It's Suzanne. Suzanne Miller. Remember, we met last month. Well, I'm back in town, but I've got poison ivy from the swimsuit layout. I told that idiot photographer that I didn't want to lie down in all those damn leaves, but he refused to listen. So...how about getting together? As soon as I stop itching. Call me."

Gabriel tipped the bottle to his lips. For some reason the voluptuous blond model seemed less appealing this

evening than she had just four short weeks ago. Maybe
it was the heat. Or perhaps he was getting old, he
mused. Now *that* was a depressing thought.

Beep. "Hello, Gabriel. This is your mother, checking to see if you're still alive. It's been nearly three weeks
since we saw you. If you're free, why don't you come
to Sunday dinner? Call me when you get a chance. A
bientôt."

Beep. "Hey, Gabriel, I probably shouldn't be talking
to you after the way you creamed me on the court this
afternoon, but something's come up. Call me as soon
as you get in, okay?"

There was a click, then a low hum as the tape in the
machine continued to unwind. Picking up the receiver, Gabriel dialed the number of the French Quarter precinct.

"What's up?" he asked when his former partner answered the phone.

"You want to tell me how come both detectives hired
by Eve Whitfield showed up at my murder scene?"
Reardon growled without preamble.

"Both detectives?"

"Richard Owens does handle the security for Whitfield Palace Hotels, right?"

"Right, but—"

"And he's supposedly the one who recommended
you to Ms Whitfield, right?"

"Right again. I figured he didn't want to take the case
because it required real detective work."

"If Owens didn't take the case, then you want to explain what he was doing at Harry Keegan's apartment
last night?"

Gabriel blinked at the question that had come from left field. "Owens was at the apartment? Last night?"

"According to the landlady, who is less than thrilled by all the cops—both private and public—who've suddenly descended on her. Seems she's on probation for passing bad paper and doesn't like all this attention."

Gabriel was becoming more confused by the minute. "How the hell could the landlady of a flophouse like that know an uptown guy like Owens?"

"One of Owens's clients is Mutual Security Insurance."

"So?"

"So Mutual Security held the city's liability policy when Keegan's landlady sued for a million dollars for injuries supposedly sustained when her car was rear-ended by an RTA bus. This was about ten years ago, back when Owens was still doing his own legwork. Well, it gets a little confusing, but according to the landlady, one night she experienced what could only be described as a miraculous recovery and left her wheelchair long enough to engage in an evening of energetic romantic pleasures. Unfortunately for her, Owens was camped out in a hotel room across the street and managed to record the action on eight millimeter film. He later testified to her healthy physical condition in court."

"I suppose you wouldn't forget someone who'd cost you a million dollars," Gabriel mused.

"Hardly. So the way I figure it, I've got one dead Fed, one phantom, brass on my back, reporters camped out on my doorstep, two private dicks hanging around the murder scene and a rich society babe who's got both PIs on retainer. I don't suppose you'd have any blinding insight to all this."

"None at all," Gabriel said honestly.

"That's what I figured," Reardon grumbled. "But it was worth a try. Oh, by the way, we ran a routine check on your client."

"Oh? Is Ms Whitfield a suspect?"

"Right now everyone including my dear old Granny Reardon is a suspect," the detective retorted. "Anyway, I thought you might like to know Ms Whitfield came up squeaky clean. She majored in something called Administration of Complex Organizations at Mount Holyoke College in Massachusetts, then picked up an MBA from Wharton. Douglas Whitfield definitely wasn't a believer in noblesse oblige—he made his darling daughter earn her way to the top, and from what I hear, now that she's there, she's damn good at her job. Word is that the lady has a heart only a polar bear could appreciate. Better watch your step with this one, old friend, or you could end up with frostbite. Talk to you later."

"Later," Gabriel agreed thoughtfully as he took another drink of beer.

He had subjective proof that Evangeline Lorraine Whitfield was not nearly as icy and controlled as she'd like people to believe. Experience had taught him that appearances were often deceiving; after what Reardon had told him about Richard Owens, Gabriel couldn't help wondering if Eve was as innocent as she seemed. Damn. He'd never liked working in the dark; it was a good way to end up dead.

Like Murphy.

Pushing himself up from the couch, Gabriel decided that he had just enough time to take a shower before starting dinner. And then he and Eve were going to sit down and get a few important things settled.

GABRIEL'S APARTMENT WAS located in a three-story brick building that sat flush against the sidewalk in the Creole style. Ornamental iron lace decorated the railings of the balconies, which were supported by decorative iron brackets. On the front of the building, a sign done in elaborate calligraphy directed her through a carriage entrance to a lushly planted courtyard. A fountain bubbled in the center of the courtyard, the captivating sound of falling water contributing to the serenity of the scene. Eve was entranced.

Although she was anxious to discover what Gabriel had learned about Harry Keegan, Eve was forced to wait until after they'd eaten to discuss the case. Insisting that dinner was not the time to discuss business, Gabriel proceeded to serve her one of the finest meals she'd ever had. And that, in a city known for its culinary arts, was definitely saying something.

Whatever other faults Gabriel had, Eve couldn't fault his cooking. The crab claws, marinated in a tangy vinaigrette, were delicious enough to make her forget her Audubon Place manners as she enthusiastically sucked the meat from the shell. She had no way of knowing that Gabriel had selected the tasty but messy appetizer precisely because it had a way of loosening guests up.

The main dish was a glorious crawfish *etouffée* served with rice, and although she swore she couldn't eat another mouthful, Gabriel managed to coax her into trying "just a bite" of bread pudding with lemon sauce and chantilly cream. By this time Eve wasn't surprised when the dessert turned out to be heavenly. Despite her best intentions, one bite led to another, and soon she was sitting on the living-room couch, certain that she'd never be able to move again.

"I can't believe I ate all that," she complained. "I probably gained twenty pounds."

Gabriel grinned. "You could gain thirty and still be gorgeous. And you know it."

Eve wasn't about to let the conversation to turn personal. "Dinner was delicious. I'm impressed."

"About time." The gleam was back in his dark eyes. Eve steadfastly ignored it.

"I've lived in New Orleans all my life, yet that's probably only the third time I've had crawfish."

"You've been missing something."

She nodded as she sipped her coffee. It was strong, hot and black with an underlying scent of chocolate. "Thank you for dinner," she said, leaning against the back of the couch. Relaxed for the first time that day, she had a sudden urge to kick off her shoes. She resisted. "It was exactly what I needed."

"Rough day?"

Eve lifted her silk-clad shoulders in a slight shrug. At Gabriel's insistence, she'd taken off her suit jacket shortly after arriving. "About average. We're having a bit of trouble with our newest hotel."

"Trouble?"

"Nothing major," she said consideringly. "Mostly cultural differences. Nothing we can't work out."

Her tone indicated she was trying to convince herself of that. Gabriel wondered what it was that could cause such furrows between those delicate brows.

Knowing the reputation of the Whitfield Palaces, it was probably something as innocuous as the dining-room staff not knowing where to put the berry spoons when they set the tables.

"I'm sure you'll handle things in your own inimitable fashion. Just like Daddy taught you to."

The frown lines deepened. "Was that a sarcastic crack?"

"Of course not. I make it a rule never to insult a guest."

"I'm not a guest. This was supposed to be a business dinner where you tell me what you've learned about Harry."

Gabriel waved her pointed suggestion away with a lazy flick of his wrist. "Business can come later—we're still in the social part of the evening. Where we get to know each other."

"What do we need to know about each other? Other than whether or not you can do a satisfactory job. And whether I can afford to pay you for doing it."

"How about your work?" he suggested. "What exactly do you do in that lofty penthouse office at Whitfield Towers?"

"A bit of everything. I read mountains of memos concerning various aspects of the company, gather the opinions of others, which creates even more paperwork, then write yet another memo detailing what I've learned to the board."

"And what does the board do?"

She surprised him by grinning. "Mostly they approve my suggestions."

"What do you do for fun?"

"Fun?"

"You know, recreation. Pleasure. Fun."

"Believe it or not, it's possible to derive pleasure from work."

"I suppose that's yet another one of life's little lessons learned at Daddy's knee."

As he watched her fingers tighten around the handle of her coffee cup, he knew he'd touched a nerve. "My father dedicated his life to building up the Whitfield Palace Hotel chain; he wanted me to follow in his footsteps."

"And do you always live your life according to what Daddy wanted?"

Eve met his eyes as she lifted the cup to her lips. "Yes."

Gabriel reminded himself that nothing would be gained by continuing to pick on her. What did he care if the woman was harboring some sort of Electra complex toward her father? She was a client. A lovely, desirable one, but a client just the same. Which meant that she was definitely off-limits.

During his first year as a detective Gabriel had fallen into what, upon later reflection, could only be called lust, although it had certainly seemed like love at the time. The woman was a pianist at one of the jazz clubs in the Quarter; he'd been assigned to a drug task force. It was only after he'd nearly lost his life in a surprise bust that turned out to be not such a surprise to the criminals that Gabriel had learned she'd only moved in with him to learn details about his work, details she passed on to her true love—one of New Orleans's most infamous cocaine dealers. From that day on, he'd kept the two aspects of his life distinctly separate.

"Tell me about your cultural problems with the hotel," he suggested, changing the subject back to its initial track before he was tempted to forget his own rule.

"Why?"

"Because I'm interested."

She studied his inscrutable features thoughtfully, finding no further sign of disapproval. "It's really funny," she said at length, leaning forward to place her empty cup on the oak-plank coffee table. "Or it would be, if it were anyone else's hotel." She shook her head at the memory of the earlier slide show. "It's just that guests at Whitfield Palace Hotels aren't used to seeing goats in the lobby."

"Goats? Where is this hotel?"

"Kathmandu."

Gabriel stared at her. "You put a Whitfield Palace in Kathmandu? Whose crazy idea was that?"

"Mine. And it's not a crazy idea. Remember in the sixties, when all the flower children were going there to find the answers to life from their gurus?"

"I think they mostly went there to blow their minds with exotic drugs."

"Well, that, too," Eve conceded. "But now all those flower children have turned into yuppies and they're running around in three-piece suits and driving BMWs and looking for exotic places to vacation."

"So Whitfield Hotels obligingly built a Palace in Kathmandu. For yippies turned yuppies who want to sleep on down pillows with ice machines on every floor."

"Exactly. Whitfield Palace Hotels exist to ensure that Americans can travel the world without suffering cultural deprivation."

"As long as they don't mind goats in the lobby."

"And rhesus monkeys frolicking in the fountains," she said with a soft sigh. "But the problems are minor—we'll solve them."

"Of course you will."

His tone was grave and strangely reassuring. Eve couldn't quite meet his admiring gaze. "We will," she repeated.

"Besides the obvious countries, you have hotels in China, Iceland, Istanbul and now Kathmandu," he said admiringly. "Is there any place left on earth where you haven't built a Whitfield Palace?"

"Bora Bora." At his surprised look Eve elaborated. "Tahiti's special. Visiting there is like traveling back in time to a romantic, mythical place, and although I realize that change is inevitable, I don't want to be the one responsible."

He smiled approvingly. "You're a special lady, Eve Whitfield."

"Not special," she corrected with a slight shrug. "Selfish. Bora Bora is the one place where I can relax and forget about my work."

Gabriel didn't respond; there was no need. Knowing Eve's workaholic tendencies, however, he couldn't help wondering what they were putting in the water on Bora Bora.

There was a small, not uncomfortable silence. Eve told herself that she should insist he tell her about Harry. That was, after all, what she'd come here for. But the evening had been so unexpectedly pleasant that she hated the thought of doing anything to spoil it. She couldn't remember the last time she'd felt so relaxed.

So she remained silent, enjoying the rich taste of her coffee and the inviting atmosphere of Gabriel's apartment.

From the clutter in his office, she had been half expecting clothes strewn over furniture from Goodwill, dust motes swirling in the air and a sink filled with dirty dishes. When the living room turned out to be surprisingly tidy, Eve had been forced to admit yet again that Gabriel was impossible to stereotype.

The outside walls were constructed of rough dark brick outlined in black. The ceiling was supported by hand-pegged oak beams and the circular stairway to the second-story loft echoed the black iron filigree work on the balcony railing. The furniture was big and over-stuffed, obviously chosen more for comfort than style, and rag rugs covered the oak planks of the floor. Although the apartment made no concessions to modern decorating trends, warmth and invitation were immediately apparent the moment a visitor stepped in the door.

"I think I like your apartment," she said, contemplating how much nicer the wide wood-burning fireplace would be, come winter, than her own practical, tidy gas one.

"But you're not sure."

She looked around. "It's a bit different from what I'm used to."

Considering the baronial atmosphere of Dixie's home at Audubon Place and Eve's own sterile environment, Gabriel decided that was a big understatement.

"A bit," he agreed. "The building used to be slave quarters. I've tried to leave it in as close a condition to the original state as possible."

"You're doing the remodeling?"

"As much as I can. Although I have to admit that my plumbing skills are nothing to write home about."

"But why doesn't the owner do his own work? Or do you moonlight as a contractor on the side?"

"A little of both. I *am* the owner."

Eve couldn't help staring. "You own this building? This entire building?"

Gabriel laughed. "Actually, the bank owns it. But they've been good enough to let me spend the rest of my life trying to pay off the mortgage. And you don't have to make it sound like the Taj Mahal, Eve. There are only three apartments, and so far this is the only one that's livable. I bought the place a couple of years ago at a foreclosure auction. It'd been sitting vacant for about ten years, unless you count all the native Louisiana wildlife that had moved in. The first thing I did was call in an exterminator. Then I began pulling away rotting wallboard and steaming away at least a hundred layers of flowered wallpaper. The entire time I kept telling myself that I was crazy."

"I can just see you," Eve murmured, imagining the room as it must have been. "A lot of people probably would've decided it wasn't worth the work."

"A lot of people didn't inherit the Bouvier stubbornness," Gabriel said easily.

Eve smiled. "Ah, yes. Grand-mère Bouvier and her sugarcane."

Gabriel's answering grin was quick and disconcertingly appealing. "Exactly. Anyway, by the time I finally got down to that brick, I was hooked on the place. It's been a love-hate relationship ever since." He gave her another one of his devastating smiles. "Your generous fee is helping to finish the bathroom next door and with any luck I'll be a landlord by spring."

It was, Eve conceded, an ambitious project. She found herself admiring Gabriel for taking it on. "When do you think you'll be finished?"

"Finished?"

She wondered why he was staring at her. "With all three apartments."

"I hope never."

"Never?"

"Never."

"I don't quite understand."

Gabriel leaned back in his chair and crossed his long legs at the ankles. "Let me explain this way: there was a fisherman who'd tried all his life to catch the largest alligator in the swamp. Finally one day he succeeded. He strung him up, and everyone came by to see the enormous alligator and praise the fisherman for his catch. But instead of feeling good, the fisherman became very sad. Because after all those years, he no longer had anything to look forward to."

"'Be careful what you wish for,'" Eve murmured.

Gabriel smiled, pleased that she'd understood. "Exactly."

As she felt the warmth of that smile all the way to her toes, Eve decided that it was definitely time to get down to business before she found herself willingly repeating last night's mistake. Folding her hands in her lap, she gave him a quietly insistent look.

"As delightful as this evening has been, I believe it's time for you to give me your report."

From her firm tone, Gabriel was astute enough to know that even though she'd been born into the family business, Eve Whitfield hadn't gotten to the top of her company by being a marshmallow. Stifling his sigh of regret, he forced his mind back to business. To Harry Keegan.

8

"FIRST OF ALL," Gabriel suggested, "why don't you tell me what kind of game you're playing."

"Game?"

"Game," he confirmed. Eve couldn't help noticing that his tone, while still pleasant, had taken on a steely edge.

"I don't know what you're talking about," she protested. "I've already told you that I'm not very good at playing games."

He studied her for a long, silent time, and although Eve knew she was being ridiculously fanciful, she felt as if the man could see all the way to her soul.

"Are you sure you haven't read *The Maltese Falcon*?" he surprised her by asking.

She forced herself to meet his probing look with a calm, level one of her own. "I told you that I haven't."

"That's funny because you're beginning to remind me more and more of the intriguing, but oh, so larcenous Miss Wonderly aka Brigid O'Shaughnessy."

"The mystery woman."

"That's her. And speaking of mysteries, how about doing me a favor and solving one that's been bothering me all evening."

Eve was more than a little confused. It was Gabriel's job to solve the mysteries. Wasn't that what she'd hired him to do? "What mystery?"

"Why you felt the need to hire both Owens and me."

She stared at him for a full ten seconds. "Owens and Martin does our security work. You knew that all along."

"True enough. But what you failed to mention is that Richard Owens is also looking for Harry."

"What?"

"Watch my lips," he instructed brusquely, growing impatient. The idea that she'd played him for a sucker from the beginning galled him more with each passing moment. Did she really think him so inept that he wouldn't find out about her subterfuge? "I want you to explain why Richard Owens is looking for Harry Keegan."

"That's ridiculous. Why would he refer me to you if he was going to take the case himself?"

"That's precisely what I've been asking myself."

Eve shook her head. "Well, it doesn't make any sense. Obviously you're wrong."

"I may be wrong about him looking for Harry," Gabriel agreed. "But I'm not wrong about him being at Harry's apartment last night."

Eve's eyes widened. "Richard Owens was at the apartment? Are you sure?"

"Reardon's got a positive ID. So the question remains, what was the guy doing there, Eve?"

Eve was silent for a moment as she digested Gabriel's accusation. Something else suddenly occurred to her; something distinctly unpalatable. "Surely you don't think that Richard was the one following us?"

"It's crossed my mind."

"But why?"

If Gabriel knew the answer to that, he wouldn't have had to suffer through dinner worrying that the lovely Eve Whitfield was playing him for a chump. "I was hoping you could shed a little light on that," he said mildly.

"But I've no idea."

She wasn't faking, Gabriel decided as an unexpected feeling of relief flooded over him. Either her surprise was genuine, or he was privileged to be watching an Academy Award-winning performance.

"Well," he said with a shrug, deciding to put the problem away until he had time to sort things out, "I guess I'll just have to do a little more detecting. Now, as for Harry, I couldn't find anyone who remembered Harry Keegan being at the state prison during those years listed on his rap sheet."

"Is that so unusual? Surely it's a large prison."

"True. But then there're those phony passports."

"Passports."

"I went back to the apartment after the police were finished going over the place."

Eve frowned. "Detective Reardon told me that the apartment had been sealed. He said that was procedure in homicide cases."

"It is."

Her frown deepened. "I'm paying you to find Harry Keegan, Gabriel. Not break the law."

"Don't worry about it—I was in and out before anyone knew I'd been there."

"Still—"

"Besides, I turned the evidence over to Joe this afternoon, so in a way you could consider my actions noth-

ing more than those of a concerned citizen assisting the
police in their investigation."

"Is that what Detective Reardon considered your little breaking and entering act?"

Gabriel grinned. "Not exactly." His ears were still
ringing from his former partner's heated curses.

"I wouldn't think so," Eve murmured. "What about
these passports?"

"I found them in the false bottom of one of the dresser
drawers."

"That was clever of you."

"Not so clever—it's a simple act of detection. You
measure the outside of the drawer, then the inside. If
there's a difference, you know you're dealing with a
false bottom."

"If it's so simple, why didn't the police do it?"

"Hey, they've got lots of cases to work on, but I've
only got this one. I can give it more time."

Eve admired his quick defense of the men he'd once
worked with. "I take it the passports belong to Harry?"

"The picture's the same, although the names and
countries of origin vary. The guy seems to have been
operating under the identities of Joseph Linsky, a com-
modities broker from Chicago, Michael Kennedy, a
member of the Irish parliament, and Otto Janzen, a
West German arms dealer."

"Harry gets around."

"Seems to."

"But?" Eve asked, hearing the irony in his tone.

"But none of those names show up on the FBI files,
either."

"There's probably a good explanation."

"Sure," he agreed. "And that explanation is that something's damn fishy in the state of Denmark."

"Rotten," she murmured.

"Whatever. Anyway, since the apartment was as clean as a whistle, it's obvious that he either forgot the passports because he was in a hurry to get out of the apartment, or something happened that didn't give him time to retrieve them before leaving. I did pick up one piece of good news," he offered encouragingly. "Harry might be a thief, but he's not a murderer."

Hope flooded into her wide blue eyes, and Gabriel knew that she was thinking of her mother. "He's not?"

"The guy in Harry's apartment was probably killed by a contract man."

"A professional killer?"

"Yeah, a guy by the name of Mad Max. He was subsequently found floating in the lake."

Her eyes were wide in her pale face. "Dead?"

"He wasn't doing the breast stroke."

Another thought occurred to her. "That man, Mad Max, went to the apartment to kill Harry, didn't he, Gabriel?"

"It looks as if that's a distinct possibility," he agreed, knowing exactly where her thoughts were headed and wishing he could do something to forestall them.

Her mouth had gone dry with unaccustomed anxiety. "We have to find him, Gabriel. If he's with Dixie when whoever wants him dead sends someone else to finish the job, then . . ."

As dread flooded into her eyes, Gabriel took her hands in his. "We'll find him," he assured her. "Believe me, sweetheart, nothing's going to happen to Dixie."

The endearment had slipped out uncensored. As she felt her blood warming beneath his fingers, Eve assured herself that it was merely a figure of speech, one a man like this undoubtedly tossed around several times a day. While she struggled to convince herself of that, Gabriel damned his incautious tongue. And reminded himself of his rule.

"There's more," he said, resolutely backing away from temptation.

"More?"

"About Harry. I found a ticket agent for TWA who remembered him buying a ticket last week."

"And this agent is positive that it was Harry?"

"Positive. She's not likely to forget the guy for a long, long time."

"What happened? Did he steal her wedding ring?"

"She'd just begun to quote the fare when her boyfriend called to say he was moving out of the apartment they'd shared for three years. Nothing personal, she was a great kid, but he'd met this other woman, etc., etc., etc. You get the picture."

Eve nodded.

"Anyway," he continued, "she kept trying to write the ticket, but her hands were shaking and she was crying, so Keegan asked the other agent to cover for her and took her to the cocktail lounge where he bought her a drink and listened sympathetically while she proceeded to enumerate every one of the louse's failings."

"That doesn't exactly sound like the behavior of a hardened criminal," Eve said thoughtfully. "If he was so anxious to get out of town, why did he take the time to calm down a distraught airline ticket agent?"

"Exactly what I was wondering," Gabriel said. "By the time she finished with what turned out to be a very long list, she had decided the jerk had done her a favor. Keegan, it appeared, agreed."

"Harry Keegan would be well acquainted with the behavior of jerks," Eve couldn't resist commenting. "He was probably only setting her up for a scam."

"I think his concern was genuine. He simply bought her a drink, provided a sympathetic ear, then purchased his ticket for the first available flight to Paris."

"He's in Paris."

"Paris," Gabriel confirmed. "Or at least he was last week. He's traveling under the name Farley Thurston-Smythe, if you can believe that."

At this point Eve decided that nothing about Harry Keegan would surprise her. "I suppose Paris is fertile ground for a jewel thief. Was it a one-way ticket?"

"Two-way. But he left the return date open. I'll be going to Paris first thing in the morning."

"Of course. I'll call my travel agent and have our tickets waiting at the airport."

"*Our* tickets?"

She could see an argument starting to swirl up in his dark eyes and prepared to hold her ground. In the beginning this had all seemed so very simple: hire a private detective to pay off Harry Keegan, then stand by to dry Dixie's tears. But she had come to accept the fact that she couldn't shift the responsibility onto someone else. Even someone earning five hundred dollars a day. Plus expenses. If anyone were going to face down Harry Keegan, it would have to be her.

"That's right. I do have a vested interest in this case,"

"I'm well aware of that. But you'll have to keep your vested interest at home. In New Orleans."

The comfortable atmosphere that had surrounded their dinner disintegrated like morning mist breaking up over Lake Pontchartrain. "I'm coming with you," Eve said quietly. Firmly.

The back and forth motion of his jaw suggested that Gabriel was grinding his teeth. "The hell you are."

Eve glanced pointedly at her watch. "If we're going to Paris tomorrow morning, we should begin making plans."

Gabriel had never been one to argue a lost cause. He knew his chances of keeping Eve Whitfield from accompanying him to Paris were on a par with his winning the Irish Sweepstakes.

"Two tickets," he agreed with a brief, dismissive shrug, surrendering to the inevitable. "We'll also need visas. And I'll need a gun permit from the French authorities."

"The French consulate officer is a friend of mine—we can have the visas by ten tomorrow morning. Meanwhile I'll have the people in our Paris office arrange for your gun permit. Is there anything else I can do for you?"

A loaded question if he'd ever heard one. Dragging his attention from the sweet curve of her lips, Gabriel forced his mind back onto the subject at hand.

"I'll want a list of all jewel robberies committed in and around Paris during the last six months," he decided. "I'll need to know what jewels were stolen, as well as names and addresses of the victims."

Eve pulled a leather-bound pad out of her purse and made a quick notation with a gold ballpoint pen. "No problem." She glanced up at him expectantly. "What else?"

Gabriel's lips quirked as he looked at her. She reminded him of an eager Thoroughbred at the starting gate. "You're really getting a kick out of all this, aren't you?"

Heaven help her, she was. Her mother's heart, perhaps even her life, was in danger, Harry Keegan was still missing, a man had been killed in his apartment, someone had tried to follow them home from that same apartment, she'd been interrogated by the police—definitely a first for someone who'd never even jaywalked—and for some reason she couldn't discern, Richard Owens had joined the cast of characters of this unbelievable drama.

The past three days had been worlds away from her usual, workaholic life-style. They'd also been undeniably exciting. But she wasn't prepared to share that secret with Gabriel.

"Or you would be," he said with the perceptiveness Eve had come to expect from the man. "If you weren't worried about Dixie."

In spite of herself, Eve decided that she was beginning to grow rather fond of Gabriel. In a cautious sort of way. "Dammit," she said with a brief shake of her head. "I really didn't want to like you."

"But?"

"I think I'm beginning to."

"Good. Because I've liked you from the beginning."

"Really?" Eve tried not to be pleased by his words. She failed. Miserably.

Gabriel found her unexpected touch of feminine vulnerability decidedly appealing. "Really. Since the moment you walked into my office looking every inch the proper Southern lady and smelling like moonlight and magnolias."

Eve couldn't quite meet his dark eyes. "You really shouldn't talk like that," she murmured distractedly. "It's not at all businesslike."

"It may not be businesslike, but it's the truth." Unable to resist any longer, he crossed to her and kissed her.

As Eve struggled to maintain some sense of equilibrium, Gabriel was drinking in her taste and wondering what it was about this woman that made it impossible to dismiss her from his mind. During the past two nights her scent had teased insistently at his senses, weaving itself into erotic dreams that had left him frustrated and aching in the morning. During the day thoughts of her had kept interrupting his work and he'd found himself daydreaming about her face—that incredible face—with its high, delicate cheekbones and wide, lushly lashed blue eyes.

"What is it about you?" he murmured as his lips skimmed up her cheekbones. "Why can't I get you out of my mind?"

Eve's own mind felt heavy, drugged, making conversation difficult. "I believe you said something about danger being an aphrodisiac," she managed finally.

Breaking the heated contact, Gabriel looked down into her warm, passion-filled eyes. "There isn't any danger tonight."

Since that first unsettling moment in his office, Eve had been discovering that anxiety and desire proved a potent combination. Unnerved and feeling faintly foolish because of it, she rose from the sofa and walked on rubbery legs across the room, where she pretended to study a dark, haunting painting.

"Isn't there?"

Good point, Gabriel conceded silently. The fact that she was perceptive as well as beautiful only made her more appealing.

"Perhaps. It's something to think about, at any rate."

"I'm paying you to think about Harry Keegan. Nothing else."

"By nothing else you mean that I'm not to think about you. That I'm not to remember how right you feel in my arms, how sweet your lips taste, how your soft, feminine body clings to mine—"

"That's precisely what I mean," she broke in, unwilling to listen to another word. As it was, his deep, caressing tone was battering away at her defenses.

She'd wrapped her arms around herself in an unconscious gesture of self-protection. Gabriel, who had admired both her intelligence and fortitude and had fantasized about the passion lurking under her coolly composed exterior, was surprised to discover that it was her vulnerability that plucked a previously undiscovered chord somewhere deep inside him. Coming up behind her, he caressed her shoulders with his palms, easing out the tension he felt there.

"I'm afraid you're asking the impossible, Eve," he murmured. "Not all of us have such rigid self-control. I can't deny thinking about you. Wondering how we'd be together. And I won't apologize for wanting you."

"I thought I wasn't your type."

It was a question he'd been asking himself from the beginning. Receiving no answer, he'd given up on it. "Tastes change. Needs and wants change."

"Not mine."

Her voice was cool, edged with frost. But as he stroked her neck with his fingertips, her skin warmed to his delicate touch. "Is it that frightening? The thought of you and me together?"

"I wouldn't know. Since I never think about it."

"Don't you?"

"No," she insisted. "I don't."

Why was he bothering to argue the point? Gabriel wondered. Granted, Eve was an attractive, desirable woman. But he knew any number of attractive, desirable women. And at least several who'd probably tumble into his bed without hesitation, including the itchy Miss July who'd left a message for him earlier. So why didn't the thought of sending Ms Uptown Eve Whitfield on her way, then picking up the phone and calling one of those willing women appeal to him?

Because he didn't want any of those women, Gabriel admitted. He wanted Eve.

Just when Eve expected Gabriel to continue, he surprised her by indicating the painting in front of them. "That's one of George Rodrigue's earlier works."

"It must be worth a great deal of money," she said, grateful for a change in subject.

"Probably. I took it as payment for some work I did a couple years ago for a family in Baton Rouge. It's *Evangeline*. You've undoubtedly heard the story— Evangeline and Gabriel were lovers separated during the odyssey of the Acadian exile. Evangeline searched all her life for Gabriel, but when she finally found him, he was married to someone else."

"I know the legend."

"I thought perhaps you did. Since you carry her name."

Eve turned and looked up at him. "How do you know that?"

"It's my business to dig out little-known facts."

"You're supposed to be investigating Harry Keegan. Not me."

"Your mother's pleased reaction to my name piqued my curiosity. When I learned that Eve was short for Evangeline, the pieces fell into place."

"Dixie's a hopeless romantic."

"And you're not."

"No." Eve's blue eyes hardened, giving him an unmistakable warning. "And the fact that my mother was reading Longfellow when she went into labor has absolutely nothing to do with us."

"Doesn't it?"

"Of course it doesn't. I hired you to find Harry Keegan. That's all. Honestly, Gabriel, for an intelligent man, you can certainly be disturbingly quixotic at times."

She made old-fashioned virtues like romanticism and chivalry sound like flaws. Gabriel decided that in Eve's mind they probably were. "I suppose so," he agreed mildly. "I'm surprised Owens didn't warn you about that when he recommended me for the job."

"Actually, he did mention something about alleged idiosyncrasies," she admitted. "But he assured me that though you have some rather unorthodox methods, you're a good detective."

"And you believed him."

"Yes. Despite your obviously mistaken impression of Mr. Owens, I respect his judgment."

"Let's not overlook Madame Leblanc's recommendation," Gabriel reminded Eve.

"What?"

"Don't tell me that you've forgotten her assertion that the man who's going to find Harry is a Scorpio."

"You were eavesdropping on a private conversation!"

"Just long enough to discover that you don't believe in Madame Leblanc's predictions."

"Of course I don't. The horrid old woman is either a raving lunatic or a fraud. Perhaps both. She spends her days tossing around chicken bones, burning candles and mixing her noxious potions and powders, for which gullible people pay ridiculous sums. No rational person would give credence to anything that crazy old witch has to say."

When Gabriel didn't respond immediately, Eve stared at him. "Don't tell me . . ." She shook her head. "No. That's too ridiculous. Even for you."

"You're probably right. It's ridiculous. Even for me."

Her eyes narrowed. "You do, don't you?"

"Believe in Madame Leblanc's predictions? No, I don't think so."

Eve was visibly relieved. It was bad enough having her mother believe in the priestess of ancient voodoo. Discovering that the man she'd hired to protect Dixie's future was a fan of Madame Leblanc's would have been too much to handle. "I'm glad to hear that."

"Although, just for the record, I do have a birthmark at the base of my spine." He flashed her a wicked grin. "Want to see it?"

"I certainly do not," Eve retorted. "You are, without a doubt, the most annoying, arrogant man I've ever met in my life, and I've had just about all of you I can take."

Once again Eve's unexpected flash of temper fascinated Gabriel. It would be a challenge to figure out how to evoke all that passion without the accompanying anger.

"Does that mean you've changed your mind about coming with me to Paris?"

Eve hated him for remaining so frustratingly calm when she was not. "Not on your life. This investigation is costing me a great deal of money, and I intend to make certain that you earn every penny of your fee."

Realizing that Gabriel might misinterpret her words, she glared up at him. His dark eyes were dancing with a devilish glee that told her they were on an identical thought wave as he pretended wounded male pride.

"Are you suggesting that I'd sell my body? Even for as hefty a fee as you're paying?"

"Are you saying you've never indulged in dalliances with your female clients?"

That was exactly what he was saying, but Gabriel had the distinct impression that Eve wouldn't believe the truth. For good reason, when he considered the way he'd been bending his own hard-and-fast rule ever since she'd waltzed into his office looking like something from the late, late show.

"I'm saying that the lady in question has to be equally eager to dally. You keep insisting that you're not."

"I'm not."

"Then what's the problem?"

Eve only wished she knew. "Nothing, I suppose." She glanced pointedly down at her watch. "Well, thank you again for dinner, but it's getting late, and I have a great deal to do if I'm going to be leaving town tomorrow. I'll call you with the flight schedule."

"Fine."

"Our tickets will be waiting at the counter."

"Fine."

"I'll also arrange for rooms at the Paris Whitfield Palace."

"Fine."

"And I suppose you'll want a rental car."

"That'd be fine."

She looked up at him suspiciously. Moonlight was streaming into the room, its gleam casting deep shadows on the angular planes of his face.

"Why are you being so agreeable all of a sudden?"

He arched his eyebrows. "I thought I'd been acting agreeably all along."

Heady perfumes from the profusion of flowers in the courtyard filled her head, making it spin. Or perhaps it was the way Gabriel was running his finger lazily over the pearl stickpin adorning her collar that was making her feel as if the earth had begun to tilt.

"I suppose that's a matter of opinion," she managed to say.

"I suppose. Is the business part of this evening over yet?"

There was no mistaking the sensual intent in his deep, velvet tone. Eve knew she should turn away. Leave. Now, before things got out of hand again. But as anticipation started to thud thickly through her veins, she found herself rooted to the spot.

"Yes."

"Good." Gabriel was smiling as he slowly, deliberately lowered his head.

9

THE KISS BEGAN as a subtle persuasion—a feathery brushing of lips, a slow stroking of his tongue against Eve's skin, his teeth nipping at her lower lip.

"It's getting late."

"Yes." Gabriel abandoned her tingling lips to press stinging kisses along the curve of her jaw.

"I have to leave."

"I know." His free hand deftly plucked at the pins in her hair.

Eve tried telling herself that it was the wine she'd had with dinner that made her feel as if the floor had begun to slip out from underneath her feet. "You can't stop me."

He tangled his fingers in the blond strands he'd released, luxuriating in their silken texture. "I wouldn't try."

Dear Lord, it wasn't the wine, Eve knew, but something much more intoxicating. More dangerous. "This is crazy."

"Insane," he agreed, burying his lips in her hair.

Little needles of heat were skimming up and down her spine, responding to a need she'd only begun to suspect she possessed after the first time Gabriel had kissed her. But had she ever felt such urgency? Had she ever been so confused?

"I hired you to find Harry," she insisted in a voice that was little more than a sigh. "That's all."

"I'll find Harry." Gabriel's hands moved from her hair to her shoulders, down her back to her hips. Their bodies met. "But we both know that isn't all that's happening here, Eve."

"Gabriel—"

"You are so soft." His tongue caressed the fullness of her lower lip. "Sweet." He moved his mouth down her throat and up again. "Sexy."

His soft voice embraced her, wrapping her in folds of lush ebony velvet. His kisses remained undemanding, his seductive touch relatively innocent. So why was her blood thickening in her veins? And why was a dark, warm ache beginning to thud insistently within her?

Her mind clouded by layers of shimmering mist, Eve decided not to search for answers now. Like Scarlett, the most practical and misunderstood of Southern women, she would ponder the problem of her relationship with Gabriel tomorrow. At the moment, however, she only wanted to luxuriate in the wondrous warmth seeping through her every cell.

Gabriel knew the exact moment Eve made her decision. Her lips turned avid, clinging to his with an urgency born of raw desire; her slender hands fretted anxiously over his chest. When her nails pressed delicately into the material of his shirt to discover the resilient flesh beneath it, Gabriel decided the hell with rules.

"You'll stay with me tonight."

Eve hesitated for the briefest of heartbeats. Then she tilted her head back and looked into his eyes. Seeing the wonder in her intimate gaze, Gabriel could have sworn that his heart had stopped.

"Yes." Smiling at his obvious relief, Eve reached up and brushed his jet-black hair off his forehead. "This always seems so much easier in the movies."

Gabriel caught her hand and kissed her fingers. "What's easier?"

"This next step."

"Next step?"

"You know . . . getting from here to—"

"The bedroom."

Embarrassed, Eve ducked her head in a brief nod.

"No problem," Gabriel assured her, lifting her in his arms. "We professional hero types are known for our fast thinking."

"I've always wanted to be swept off my feet." She sighed happily, resting her head against his shoulder.

"Gabriel Bouvier Investigations aims to please."

As he carried her into his bedroom, Eve felt as if she were floating. She felt lighter than air. Free. She laughed softly as she nibbled gently on his earlobe.

"I'm glad you find this so humorous," Gabriel complained as he placed her on the bed. The sheets still carried his scent from the night before; Eve had a sudden urge to wrap herself in the fragrant folds of navy percale. "Didn't your mama ever teach you that it's dangerous to laugh at a man in my condition?"

She reached up and pressed her palm against his cheek. "I wasn't laughing at you," she assured him. "I was laughing because I felt so good." She let her fingers linger around the jutting line of his jaw. "You make me feel so good."

The mattress sighed, then settled as he sat down beside her and drew her into his arms. "That's what I want to do. That's what I've wanted to do since the beginning."

"I know. I was afraid of you," she admitted softly. "Of my feelings toward you . . . in the beginning."

"And now?"

"And now I want you." Want was too mild a word. Yearn, crave, need. None of the paltry substitutions that entered her mind even came close to what Eve was feeling. All she knew was that if Gabriel didn't make love to her soon, she'd go insane.

The admission was all he'd been waiting for.

With hands that were not as steady as he would have liked, he proceeded to undress her. The details were blurred as Eve luxuriated in the pure pleasure of cloth being whisked over her warm skin. She was vaguely aware of her brown suede pumps dropping to the stone floor, followed in turn by her yellow silk blouse and slim linen skirt.

Gabriel's eyes flamed as he gazed down at her, clad only in an ivory bra so sheer it could have been spun from cobwebs and a skimpy pair of silk bikini panties.

"You are so beautiful," he murmured huskily as he cupped the soft weight of one breast in his hand.

Eve gasped as his mouth warmed her flesh through the ivory lace. In that brief blinding moment all her doubts disintegrated, all the reasons it wasn't wise for her and Gabriel to be together this way fled her mind, leaving her only with a need to touch. To be touched. To love. And to be loved.

"I want to touch you," she said, her hands slipping beneath his shirt to move in heated circles against his bare back.

"Oh, sweetheart, I thought you'd never ask." He rose from the bed just long enough to undress. Then he was back, lying beside her, murmuring words of encouragement as her hands explored the rigid lines of his body, first tentatively, then with more assurance.

An early-evening rain had brought a temporary cooling relief, and the air was rich with the heady scent of tropical flowers—jasmine, gardenia and honeysuckle. The summer moonlight wrapped the bedroom in ribbons of silvery light while the bluesy sounds of a saxophone drifted on the perfumed night air like a lover's sighs.

"At the risk of destroying the moment, there's something I need to know," he said, punctuating his words with soft, enticing kisses against her lips.

Her hand was pressed against his chest. His skin was warm, his heartbeat strong but every bit as rapid as her own. "I promise to respect you in the morning," she murmured, trailing her fingers through the crisp ebony curls on his chest.

"That's nice to know, although it wasn't exactly what I was worrying about." As her exploring touch went dangerously lower, hovering at his hip, Gabriel drew in a deep breath and caught the treacherous hand before it succeeded in destroying the last vestige of his control. "It's not that I have anything against children—in fact, I've often thought I'd make a pretty good father—but I've also always believed it should be a joint decision. Are you protected, Eve?"

Color rose in her cheeks as she realized that she, a successful, intelligent career woman, had been caught behaving like a love-crazed, irresponsible teenager. "No. I'm sorry, Gabriel, I don't know what came over me, but I just didn't think. You must think I'm a terrible tease. Or worse."

He couldn't resist smiling at her forlorn expression. "Shh," he whispered, pressing his lips against hers once again for a long, drugging kiss. "It's okay." He left her for only the length of time it took to retrieve a foil-wrapped package from the bedside table.

Immensely relieved and strangely moved that despite his rising sexual hunger, Gabriel had remained considerate of her safety, Eve welcomed him with open arms. His moist flesh was taut, lean, hard—absolutely male. Hers was soft, silky, perfumed—unquestionably female. Flesh to flesh, male and female, rigid angles to delicate curves, they complemented each other even as they sought to drive each other mad.

Eve's skin tingled with insistent longing, but she resisted, taking an agonizingly long time to kiss her way through the dark hairs arrowing down his torso. Gabriel's response was a low growl deep in his throat as his tongue caressed her nipples, treating each in turn to a slow, lingering torment that created eddies of escalating need between her thighs.

Words were no longer necessary, desires were telegraphed by hands. By lips. By quiet sighs and low moans. He touched and her body burned. She tasted and his skin flamed.

His lips rushed over her—hot, stinging kisses that threatened to drive her to the very edge of reason. Then beyond. Heat from his mouth seeped into her bloodstream, causing searing flashes of blinding pleasure. The sheets were hot and tangled under her back; the sultry, moon-silvered air surrounding them was thickened with the fire and smoke of their blazing passion.

Her heated flesh gleamed like satin and felt like silk. Gabriel's mouth lingered at the inside of first one thigh, then the other, creating needs that grew increasingly unbearable. When his tongue delicately flicked against the tingling pink bud, Eve was jolted by a violent, instantaneous climax.

She was still trembling from the intensity of her response when Gabriel demonstrated that he'd just begun. With clever fingers and wicked lips he drove her higher, relentlessly bringing her to crest after shuddering crest until her body hummed with a thousand pounding pulses.

While she was still gasping for breath, her love-slick body limp and pliant, Gabriel thrust into her, making them one. Stunned that she could experience such blinding passion yet again, and so soon, Eve moved with him, faster and faster, until the end finally came— an end that was as explosive as it was wonderful—and they were catapulted into a relationship that neither had been prepared to accept.

INFUSED WITH A DEEP, heavy languor, Eve lay with her cheek against Gabriel's chest, drinking in the musky scent of his skin and listening to the steady thudding of his heartbeat as it settled back to normal. As for her own heart, Eve wasn't sure it would ever be the same.

She had never offered herself so blatantly to a man before; she'd never given so freely, so openly of herself. Nor had she ever wanted to. It was not that her limited sexual experience was due to any lack of opportunity; she'd politely rebuffed her share of potential suitors over the years. The simple truth was that sex had never been an overwhelming force in her life. Indeed, the past few years she had been perfectly content to pour her energies into her work, receiving satisfaction from a job well done.

Her father had brought her up to be strong and independent—a carbon copy of himself. For twenty-nine years Eve had kept her emotions on a tight rein, opting for practicality over passion, logic over love. Until now. Until Gabriel Bouvier.

She'd never met a man capable of triggering such a volatile sense of sexual awareness. With a single look, a mere touch, he could arouse her to desperation, inflaming passions she'd never realized existed within her. These unruly feelings that Gabriel evoked were proving every bit as alarming as they were thrilling. Some deep-seated instinct told Eve that if she wanted to distance herself from the man whose wide hand was lazily caressing her body, she'd have to do it now.

"Regrets already?" Gabriel asked as she made a move to escape the rumpled bed. His fingers tightened ever so slightly on her hip at the same time as he flung a leg over both of hers, effectively holding her hostage.

"Not at all," she insisted, not quite truthfully. "But it's late—if we're flying to Paris tomorrow, we'll both need a good night's sleep."

His eyelids opened lazily to give her a mildly amused glance. "I never figured you for a lady who'd go back on her word, Evangeline."

Whitfield pride stiffened her spine. "I'm not."

"What about your promise to stay here?" His lips brushed against her shoulder with the lightest of touches. "With me. All night long."

She damned her incautious tongue even as she felt her skin warm to his feathery kisses. "Really, Gabriel, surely you're not going to hold me to a promise made in the heat of passion."

"A promise is a promise," he murmured playfully as he stroked her body in a way that was anything but soothing.

"Gabriel—"

"Shhh." He pressed his lips against hers, and a shaft of heat shot through them.

Languor was fast giving way to need. Eve struggled to maintain her equilibrium even as her world was fast changing. "This won't ever work," she protested unsteadily. "We're too different, you and I."

He trailed his fingers over her breasts. *"Vive la différence."*

"I'm not talking about physical differences," she insisted. It was suddenly vitally important that he understand. "I'm referring to our life-styles."

Gabriel sighed as he lifted his head and looked down into her serious face. "Our life-styles?"

"I'm a very serious person—I always have been. While you, on the other hand..." Her voice trailed off as she tried to choose her words carefully.

Gabriel knew where her train of thought was leading. Just as he knew her appraisal of their situation was wrong. He didn't know what was taking place between them, but whatever it was, it was probably the best thing that had happened to either one of them in a very long time.

"While I live in a world of adolescent fantasies, spending all my time playing cops and robbers," he helped her out.

She felt the treacherous color rising in her cheeks and wondered why she'd never noticed this unfortunate propensity for blushing. "That's not exactly what I was going to say."

He looked calmly into her embarrassed face. "Of course not. Your description of my indolent life would have undoubtedly been far more discreet. But no less censorious."

Despite his casual tone, a flash of angry pride appeared fleetingly in his dark eyes. It disappeared so quickly that had Eve not been watching intently, she would have missed it entirely. She'd seen that look once before—in her office when she'd accused him of wasting her time and money playing handball.

"Now who's jumping to conclusions?"

"You can't deny that you don't approve of the way I make my living," Gabriel countered quietly. Too quietly, Eve thought.

"It's not for me to approve or disapprove."

"That's why you looked as if you'd taken a wrong turn at Saks and ended up in slum city when you walked in my office door. Admit it, sweetheart, if you hadn't been so anxious to protect your mother by buying off her lover, you'd have turned tail and run right back to the insular safety of that sterile office in Whitfield Towers. Or your equally austere apartment. Where you can avoid any unsavory contact with the real world."

That hurt. Head high, perfectly shaped blond brows arched, she glared at him. "That's a cruel and untrue thing to say. Of course I was nervous—I'd never hired a private detective before. But that's all it was."

The icy fury in her eyes was in direct contrast to the warmth of the woman who'd turned to flaming silk in his arms only a few minutes earlier. Gabriel found himself fascinated yet again by both aspects of her personality and wondered why the hell they were wasting time arguing when they could be making love.

He pulled her closer, his arms tightening around her when she tried to resist. "One question, Evangeline," he insisted quietly. "Surely that's not too much to ask." He shifted her into a more comfortable position. "Not after all the hours I slaved over a hot stove cooking you an authentic Cajun dinner after spending a long, hard day tracking down your mother's errant jewel-thief lover."

Furious that he was holding her against her will and appalled by the way his hands, pressed against her naked back, were making her pulse race once again, Eve fought to keep her voice steady. "Are you trying to make me feel guilty?"

"Would it work?"

"Not on your life."

Gabriel slipped his leg between hers. "Are you sure about that?"

Heat was building between her thighs—a slow, simmering warmth that Eve did her best to ignore. "Positive . . . Dammit, Gabriel," she complained, slapping at his hand as it began caressing her back from her shoulder to the flare of her hip, "didn't anyone ever tell you that you can't always get your own way?"

"All the time, but I try not to listen." He pressed his lips into the love-tousled clouds of her blond hair.

She'd never met a man as obstinate and single-minded as this one. Unless it was her father. Once again the resemblance between the two men flashed through her mind. Once again she dismissed it as ridiculous. Knowing that Gabriel was more than willing to hold her hostage in his bed until she gave in to his demands, Eve decided the sensible thing would be to answer his ridiculous question, then get dressed and leave this apartment. Before she got in over her head.

"All right," she agreed. "One question."

"What is it about me that you find so offensive?"

She stared up at him. "But I don't find you at all offensive, Gabriel."

"Then why are you in such a hurry to rush off?"

"I told you—"

"I know. We've got a busy day tomorrow. And that's about the lousiest excuse I've ever heard for turning something indescribable into a cheap, one-night—correction, make that a cheap, one-hour—stand."

"I certainly didn't mean you to take it that way."

"Oh, no? How would you feel if it were the other way around? If I had been the one who promised to stay, took whatever you had to offer, then afterward tried to leap out of your bed as if the sheets were on fire."

Put that way, her actions were decidedly unpalatable. Eve closed her eyes briefly. "I'd feel terrible," she admitted quietly.

"Used?"

"That, too. I'm sorry."

"Apology accepted and appreciated." His mouth brushed hers. Lightly. Tantalizingly. "Have I told you that I love the way you taste?"

This time it was need, not shame, that made her close her eyes. Feeling much, much weaker than she should have been, she put her arms around his neck and linked her fingers. "I don't need the words," she protested in a whisper.

His mouth skimmed up her cheek, loitering warmly at her temple. "Perhaps *you* don't need the words," he murmured huskily, drinking in the scent of flowers in her hair. "But ever since meeting you, I've discovered that I do... You taste like passion." His lips moved back down her face, lingering for a blissful, suspended moment on hers before continuing down her throat. "Warm, sultry."

He could feel the rising pleasure seeping through her as her body softened in a silent submission he knew was deceptive, remembering the feminine aggression she'd brought to their earlier lovemaking. He'd bring her to that point again, he knew, when her hunger would be every bit as desperate as his own. But for now, for this glorious, immeasurable moment, he was content to take his time, drawing those soft, pleased little sighs from her parted lips.

"Intoxicating." His tongue caressed her aching breasts in slow, wet, wonderful strokes that left her gasping when his mouth moved on. "A man could get drunk from the sweet taste of your skin alone."

She was trembling for him, stunned by a passion that had returned in full force. Fire skimmed along her skin wherever his mouth lingered—her breasts, the ultra-sensitive back of her knees, the tingling flesh of her inner thighs. It was torment. Torment mingled with an exquisite pleasure that was like nothing she'd ever known.

Madness surged through her veins, greed and hunger swirled in her head, making her dizzy as she reached for him, her avid lips and impatient hands moving over him, teasing, tempting, thrilling. Then Eve slipped deftly out of his arms and reversed their positions, sprawling wantonly across his body as her hands and mouth grew increasingly bolder. When her lips lovingly caressed the part of him that was aching for release, his sanity shattered. Grasping her hips, he gave himself over to the passion. And to her.

Eve's soft cry was one of astonished pleasure as they joined, and Gabriel paused for a long, delicious time, savoring the sweetness of the moment. Then they began to move, neither knowing nor caring who set the pace as they raced toward oblivion.

THE BIRDS WOKE HER. Eyes closed, Eve could feel the warmth of the early-morning sun on her face as she reached groggily for her bedside clock. When her exploring fingers failed to locate it, she sat up and opened her eyes, disoriented. Then, as she stared around the bedroom, taking in the rough brick walls and timbered ceilings, comprehension dawned.

Her alarm clock wasn't in its usual position inches away from the bed because she wasn't in her bed. She was in Gabriel's. And last night hadn't been an amazingly sensual dream. It had been all too real, as the vague ache in her muscles attested.

What had she done? And even more important, what was she going to do now? Her mind whirling, she listened carefully for signs of Gabriel's presence in the apartment—coffee perking, a radio playing, water running—and heard none. Relieved, she sprang from the bed, gathered her scattered clothing and escaped into the bathroom. With any luck she could be back in her own apartment before he returned from wherever it was he'd disappeared to.

As HE RAN through the deserted streets of the French Quarter, Gabriel was wide awake, pumped full of energy. He felt strong, invincible, able to leap tall buildings in a single bound. In short, he felt terrific. And there was not one doubt in his mind that the reason for his enormous sense of well-being was the woman he'd left sleeping in his bed.

A warm wave of possessiveness swept through him as he remembered how she'd looked, her blond hair strewn across his pillow like strands of spun silk. The delicate little circles under her eyes had testified that she'd gotten no more sleep last night than he had; her softly bruised pink lips had shown that she'd been long and thoroughly kissed.

He heard someone call his name. Glancing around, he waved a hearty good-morning to the elderly street vendor setting up his snowball stand. Gabriel guessed that the shaved ice desserts were probably more popular than ever these days; it was good to know that someone was profiting from the heat wave.

He'd no sooner turned the corner than his thoughts returned to Eve. Eve and Paris. Now there was an unbeatable combination. Motivated by that appealing thought, he sprinted the last half mile back to the apartment.

10

EVE WAS ON HER WAY OUT Gabriel's front door when he came skidding to a halt directly in front of her.

The man was, Eve thought weakly, too much of an assault on her senses first thing in the morning. He was wearing a ragged gray T-shirt with LSU Athletic Department emblazoned on it. The shirt had been cut off at his torso, exposing ebony hair that disappeared into the waistband of a pair of navy running shorts. His body was lean and hard and brown, the long, whipcord muscles glistening with a fine film of perspiration in the bright morning light.

Against her will, desire flared. Digging her fingernails into her palms, Eve managed, with extreme effort, to bank it. "Good morning."

Her greeting was definitely not what Gabriel had been expecting; cool and stiffly polite, it brought to mind afternoon tea at the Windsor Court, a local hotel that served English teas. No longer the wonderfully wanton woman who'd driven him to distraction all night long, Eve had metamorphosed into a nononsense, humorless businesswoman. She was wearing her tailored clothes like a protective suit of armor, and her hair, which he'd delighted in running his fingers through while they'd made love, was back in its intricate twist at the nape of her neck.

Attempting to bridge the gulf that had sprung up between them, Gabriel reached out and touched her cheek. "Morning, *chérie*. Are you hungry? Let's go out for breakfast and then—"

"I don't eat breakfast," she interrupted, wanting to return to her office in Whitfield Towers, where she felt in control of her life.

"How about coffee and *beignets*?" he suggested enticingly. "We can drop by the Café du Monde, sit outside and take advantage of the Mississippi River breeze."

He shouldn't look this good, Eve groaned inwardly. His hand shouldn't feel so right on her skin. His dark eyes, smoldering with uncensored desire, should not make her want to forget about her work and her mother and Harry Keegan and spend the rest of her life making love with this man who was every bit as wrong for her as she was for him. She shook her head with very real regret as she backed away from his tender touch.

"Thank you for the offer, but I have work to do before we leave. I've contacted my travel agent, and we're booked on the one o'clock flight to New York, then the night flight to Paris."

"Your travel agent must keep early office hours."

"I called her at home. Oh, and we can pick up our visas anytime after ten-thirty this morning."

"I'm impressed; you must have the consul's home number, as well."

"Of course. Whitfield Palace Hotels does a great deal of—"

"Business in France," Gabriel concluded for her.

She frowned at his dry tone. "That's right."

The gulf was widening more and more the longer this conversation continued. Gabriel wanted to scoop her up, carry her into the bedroom, strip off that damnedly proper business suit and reveal the witch he knew was hiding deep inside that cool, calm exterior. Knowing that such antediluvian antics would only result in Eve's firing him, and thus cutting off any valid excuse they had to be together, he shoved his hands into the pockets of his shorts to keep from touching her again.

"May I ask a personal question?"

Eve eyed him warily. This was precisely how he'd managed to keep her here the last time she'd said she wanted to leave. "Surely you learned everything you needed to know about me last night." The words were no sooner out of her mouth than Eve realized she'd made a grave tactical error. Remembered passion darkened his eyes to gleaming ebony.

"Almost everything," he murmured. "What I can't understand is what you have against pleasure."

"That's ridiculous." After last night how could he ask such a question?

He lifted a dark brow. "Is it? I'm not talking about sex, Eve. I'm talking about life."

"Funny, from the way you kept trying to seduce me, I would have thought sex *was* your life," she snapped, tired of his pushing her into emotional corners.

"Dammit, that's not what I'm talking about, and you're intelligent enough to know it."

Frustrated by the way his good mood was disintegrating, Gabriel took her by the shoulders, as if to shake her. His flare of temper caught them both by surprise, and as Eve stared up into his rigid face, Gabriel regained control and loosened his grip on her.

"I'm sorry," he said. "I didn't mean to hurt you."

He hadn't. Not yet. But he could, Eve considered, if she allowed last night's mistake to continue. "You didn't. But I really should be going."

"In a minute. First tell me when you last took time to enjoy the simple things in life—a morning sunrise, the feel of soft summer rain on your face, popcorn at the zoo, the heady scent of roses in the City Park gardens—"

She held up her hand. "You can stop any time, Gabriel. I get your drift."

"And?"

It was so easy for him. He thought nothing of spending his afternoons watching baseball games—now *there* was a frivolous pastime—instead of searching out business. And then, when potential clients did him the favor of walking in the door of his less-than-impressive office, he continued to maintain his independent outlook toward life by only taking cases that appealed to him.

If her father had done only the work he enjoyed, if she omitted all the unpleasant, repetitive tasks she was forced to plod through on a daily basis, Whitfield Palace Hotel's worldwide empire wouldn't exist. She'd be lucky to be operating a rundown motel with patched muslin sheets, televisions bolted to the dressers, and a candy machine that routinely stole guests' change as the closest thing to room service.

"I have an extremely demanding life," she said evenly.

"I'm well aware of that. But is it a full life?"

"I manage to keep busy; my days are quite full."

"Working."

She met his vaguely censorious look with a long, level one of her own. "It may come as a surprise to discover that some people find work extremely satisfying. Even fulfilling."

"I know that. You happen to be looking at one of them."

She didn't bother to keep her skepticism from showing. Instead of being irritated by her blatant disbelief, Gabriel decided that Douglas Whitfield's dutiful daughter was in dire need of a dose of fun. And he intended to see that she received it, no matter how hard or how long she fought him. Although patience had never been his long suit, years of painstaking investigative work had taught him that success didn't always come easily.

"I'll make you a proposition."

Eve crossed her arms over her breasts. "Now why doesn't that surprise me?"

Gabriel ignored her dig. "I'll find Harry Keegan if you allow yourself to experience some of the pleasures Paris has to offer while we're there."

"You can't actually expect me to enjoy myself when my mother's heart and possibly her very life are in danger because of her involvement with Harry. My God, Gabriel, don't you take anything seriously?"

I take you more seriously that I ever expected to, Gabriel could have answered. "I take my work very seriously," he said instead. His fingers cupped her chin, lifting her frowning gaze to his. "Believe me, Eve, we'll find Harry. And when we do, we'll work something out to keep Dixie from being any more emotionally wounded than she absolutely has to be. But in the meantime, all I'm asking is that you open yourself up to the pleasurable things in life."

"Stop and smell the roses," she muttered, repeating the advice Dixie was always giving her.

Actually, now that she thought about it, her mother and Gabriel were alike in many ways. It was too bad they'd been born a generation apart; they probably would have made an ideal couple. The match would likely have been more compatible than the marriage between Dixie and her father had been. And much, much more suitable than an affair between her and Gabriel.

"Something wrong with that?" he asked.

"What makes you think I haven't already done that?" she complained. "I'll have you know I cut a meeting short last night in order to have dinner with you."

"And did Whitfield Palace Hotels fall apart because you took an evening off?"

"That's not the point. Don't you see? Before I met you, I'd never have recessed a meeting early. And I definitely would not have dropped everything in order to go rushing off to Paris to track down a convicted jewel thief."

It took an effort, but Gabriel managed not to smile at Eve's earnest expression. "Are you saying I'm a bad influence on you?"

"Of course not." She closed her eyes, garnering strength. "But I've been acting totally out of character ever since all this began, and I can't understand why."

"Why don't you stop worrying about it and simply take things as they come," Gabriel suggested gently. "How does that sound?"

Take things as they come. Eve was certain it was precisely the way Gabriel went through life. While she, on the other hand, never began a day without a detailed list of things she wished to accomplish, never entered into any venture without a distinct goal.

"It sounds unpredictable."

"That's the idea, *chérie*." He gave her a satisfied kiss that made her toes curl in her brown pumps.

"I'd better be going," she said when she could speak again. "I still have to change before going into the office."

"Afraid that if you show up at work in the same suit you wore yesterday, the troops might figure out their commander in chief spent the night away from home?"

Eve's newly discovered temper flared at his condemning tone. "A CEO who sleeps around is not exactly the image I wish to convey."

"Probably cause Whitfield stock to take a nosedive." Although his tone was calm, his dark eyes were not. "And for the record, Evangeline, you were not 'sleeping around.' You were making love. With me." That said, he placed his hand lightly on her back. "Let's go—I'll drive you home."

"I have my car."

"So I'll drive you home in your car. Despite what you think of me, I'm not the type of man who sends a lady home alone."

Some perverse curiosity made her wonder exactly how many women spent the night at Gabriel's apartment during an average week. Or month. When she found herself experiencing something that felt too much like jealousy for comfort, Eve returned her thoughts to more practical matters.

"If we take my car, how will you get home?"

He shrugged. "No problem—I'll take a cab."

"We seem to be spending a lot of time switching cars," she said, thinking of the other night when it had been she who'd left her Jaguar at Dixie's.

"So move in with me and we can carpool."

The suggestion, which was as much a surprise to Gabriel as it was to Eve, sounded eminently attractive. He found himself waiting for her answer.

"The city transportation department would love us—it'd take one more car off the roads at rush hour. And speaking of rush hours, if you're going to insist on playing the gentleman by seeing me to my door, perhaps you ought to get dressed. My doorman definitely isn't used to my arriving home in the morning with half-dressed men."

He hadn't really believed that she'd give in to that momentary temptation he'd watched move across her face. But there had always been an outside chance that she might.

"That's a relief," he said, pressing a quick, hard kiss against her lips before going into the apartment to shower.

Eve remained where she was, her fingers pressed against her lips where she continued to feel the heat for a long, long time.

"OH, MY GOD!"

Thirty minutes later Eve was staring at what could only charitably be called a mess. Her usually immaculate living room looked as if it had suffered an earthquake, followed in rapid succession by a hurricane.

Bleakly, her eyes took in the paintings ripped from the walls, their frames broken by the intruders who had apparently searched beneath their backing. The silk upholstery on her sofa had been slashed, the stuffing strewn over the alabaster carpeting like unmelted snow. Her books, including the first editions that her father had given her each year since her thirteenth birthday, had been torn apart. Pages were littered everywhere, along with the contents of her desk.

The scene was no less disconcerting in the bedroom, where her mattress had been slashed and dresser drawers pulled out and overturned. Eve couldn't quite stifle the soft cry when she saw how her clothing had been flung about.

"Why?" she whispered as she plucked a lacy, seafoam teddy from the doorknob. "They didn't take my jewelry," she said, glancing at a string of pearls and an opal ring lying forlornly amid the rubble. "Why would anyone do such a thing?"

Actually, Gabriel had a few ideas of his own along those lines, and none of them was very pleasant. "We need to call the cops," he insisted, taking the teddy from her. The touch of her hand and the smooth satin reminded him of how her skin had felt while they were making love, with one important exception. Last night her skin had been warm. At the moment her whiteknuckled hands were like ice. "Reardon should see this."

The thought of dealing with the police for the third time in as many days was unpalatable enough, but Gabriel's suggestion that they call the detective who was heading up a murder task force made Eve's blood run cold.

"Surely you can't think this has anything to do with Harry. Or that murdered man," she insisted, sinking down on her shredded mattress when her knees threatened to give way. "It's a burglary. Nothing more."

He shook his head as he gingerly used the teddy to pick up the telephone. He didn't want to take the chance of smudging any fingerprints the intruders might have inadvertently left, but he also didn't want to leave Eve alone in the middle of this disaster area. And from the way all the color had fled her face at the mention of his former partner, he wasn't certain she'd be capable of accompanying him down to the lobby.

"Honey," he argued gently as the phone rang on the other end of the line, "you're the one who pointed out that nothing of value was taken. Which means that the people who trashed this place were probably the same guys who followed us the other night."

"But why?"

"They were obviously looking for something that would lead them to Harry. Maybe they think you know more about Keegan's activities than you do. Like what he's up to, or where he is."

"Well," Eve decided, "that certainly eliminates Richard Owens from the list of suspects."

"Why?"

"Because the man's a consummate professional, and he comes from one of New Orleans's oldest families. He'd be incapable of anything like this." An unpalatable thought suddenly occurred to Eve. "Dixie," she whispered, her eyes wide with fright.

"I'm already ahead of you on that one. Joe," he said, turning his attention to the man who'd answered his precinct telephone. "We've got a problem. But first you need to get a black and white out to Audubon Place."

Despite her swirling head, Eve was impressed when Gabriel calmly described the situation in as few words as possible. Richard Owens had been right; Gabriel Bouvier was very, very good at his job.

When he'd finished his conversation, Gabriel turned his attention to Eve. The color was returning to her face, and the fear he'd seen in her eyes was beginning to turn into a slow, seething anger.

"Can I get you anything? A drink? Some aspirin?"

"No. Thanks."

"Are you sure?"

Eve couldn't remember the last time anyone had looked at her with such gentle concern. "Positive." She realized that once again Gabriel had witnessed a distressing display of helplessness. But instead of feeling embarrassed by nearly falling apart in front of him, she felt a mellow warmth flowing through her because of his strong, reassuring presence. "I take that back," she said softly, her gaze fixed on his face. "There is something you can do for me."

"Anything."

She held out a hand that trembled slightly, her blue eyes eloquent in their need. "Hold me," she asked with a gentle sigh. "Please hold me—just for a minute."

Her softly spoken words turned Gabriel suddenly and unexpectedly speechless. It wasn't passion that caused a lump to rise suddenly in his throat. Nor desire. It was simple affection. Simple? he asked himself as he sank down beside her and drew her to him. Hardly.

Eve closed her eyes as she rested her forehead against his firm, solid shoulder. His arms, wrapped around her, were strong and reassuring. A woman could feel safe locked in these arms. Secure. But could she also remain free?

Her hard-won autonomy was vital to her very existence; she could never have subjugated her own essential needs for a man as Dixie had done. With her gaze directed steadfastly to her goals, Eve had never once regretted her decision not to marry and have children, as so many of her friends had done. The rewards for her unwavering dedication had been a successful career at Whitfield Palace Hotels, a sleek, expensive car, an art collection that appreciated with each passing day, shelves filled with first editions, travel all over the world and a stylish, expensive condominium overlooking the lake.

Opening her eyes, Eve stared bleakly around at the ruins of the apartment that had twice been featured in the Sunday paper's *Life-style* section and couldn't help wondering, for the first time in her life, if the rewards had been worth the sacrifice.

Gabriel rested his cheek against the smooth crown of her head. Her fingers were kneading unconsciously at the muscles of his back, and as he felt her trembling begin to subside, he was surprised to find that holding her brought a contentment that was decidedly in contrast to the passion of their lovemaking.

It was strange, Eve mused, as a feeling of peace settled over her like a warm, comforting blanket. He'd gotten under her skin from the beginning, chipping away at her inhibitions, discovering unsettling emotions she'd been unaware of possessing. Her unwilling

attraction to Gabriel had hit her full force and unexpectedly, like a lightning bolt out of a clear blue sky.
Their lovemaking had been the same—wildfire and
smoke, storm and fury. She never would have thought
it possible to spend a quiet moment with him. But it was
possible. And it was wonderful.

The gentle mood was shattered by a familiar voice
calling his name. "Hey, Gabe," Joe Reardon shouted,
"where are you?"

Muttering a soft oath, Gabriel tightened his arms
around Eve, hoping that her own soft sigh meant she
was no more thrilled with being interrupted than he had
been. "In here," he called as he released her and stood
up. "Duty calls," he murmured unenthusiastically.

Eve's expression held the same regret. "Thank you,
Gabriel. For. . ." Her hand fluttered in a vague, inartic-
ulate gesture. "Everything," she finally whispered.

Her interview with Joe Reardon took less than ten
minutes. Once again Eve wished she could be more
helpful as her cursory examination failed to turn up any
missing items. After assuring the detective that she had
absolutely no idea who would want to do such a thing,
she forced her whirling mind to concentrate on the
myriad loose ends that had to be tied up at Whitfield
Palace Hotels before she left for Paris that afternoon.

EVE HAD EXPECTED her mother to be distraught at the
sudden appearance of uniformed police at her Audubon Place home. Instead, when she and Gabriel
stopped by the house on their way to the office, Dixie
appeared to be the least upset of all of them.

"They were just possessions, Eve," she pointed out
calmly. "Possessions can always be replaced. Thank

heaven no one was hurt. How are you holding up, dear? I do hope this unfortunate business hasn't upset you too badly."

"I'm fine."

They were sitting out on the terrace. Nearby, in the garden where Dixie hoped to have her wedding, the roses were in full bloom, their soft fragrance mingling with the scent of newly mown grass. Douglas Whitfield had created such a lovely, peaceful environment for his wife; Eve hated Harry Keegan for bringing death and danger into such an idyllic setting.

"Of course you are," Dixie said reassuringly. "Your father always said you had nerves of steel." She studied Eve and Gabriel judiciously over the crystal rim of her ice tea glass for a moment. "Poor dears, you both look so tired," she said. "Why don't you spend the day here? You can swim, play tennis, lie in the sun, whatever you feel like doing. I'll ask Ethel to make a nice shrimp salad for lunch and—"

"I'd love that, Dixie," Eve broke in. "But I'm going out of town."

"On business?"

"Not exactly," Eve hedged.

There was no disguising the hope shining in Dixie's violet eyes. "It's Harry, isn't it? Gabriel's found him."

"Mother—"

"Eve, regardless of your well-meaning but misguided attempts to shield me from the real world, I am an adult," Dixie retorted, her voice uncharacteristically sharp. A moment later her tone softened. "Darling, I love Harry and I'm the one who suggested hiring a detective to find him in the first place. I deserve to know what's happening."

Eve recognized the tone. In her own gentle way Dixie could, when sufficiently provoked, be an irresistible force. Possessing a fair amount of tenacity herself, Eve had always appreciated the trait in others. Until now.

Eve could feel Gabriel's gaze on her face and knew he'd decided that the time had come to tell the truth. Because she recognized the legitimacy of Dixie's complaint, and most of all because she loved her mother, Eve relented. But only to a point.

"We think Harry's in Paris," she admitted reluctantly. "We're leaving this afternoon."

"I had no idea Harry had family in Paris," Dixie mused. "Imagine that."

"Imagine," Eve murmured, refusing to meet Gabriel's eyes.

"Excuse us for a moment, Dixie," he said smoothly, taking Eve by the elbow and pulling her up from the table.

"What do you think you're doing?" Eve complained as he practically dragged her down the garden path.

"Trying to talk some sense into you. Your mother may be a little scatterbrained, but she isn't stupid. How long do you plan to keep her in the dark?"

A fat yellow-and-black bumblebee buzzed lazily over a snow-white blossom; nearby a hummingbird hovered, its delicate wings fluttering as it drank the nectar from a scarlet tea rose. Both went unnoticed as Eve glared up at him.

"With any luck, forever. Or at least until we find Harry and pay him off."

"It isn't going to be that easy, and you damn well know it." Gabriel's fingers tightened on her arm when Eve tried to shake off his hold. "Whatever Harry's mixed up in, he's not in it alone. That mess in your apartment proves that he's already involved you, Eve. What if Dixie's next?"

Part of her hated him for being right. The other part had to admit that he was. "Oh, God," she groaned, "this is getting so complicated."

"I know." He ran his hands up her arms and rested them on her shoulder. "I can arrange for someone to stay at the house while we're gone," he said. "Just in case. But you're going to have to tell Dixie the truth, *chérie*. It's the only way."

Eve closed her eyes and rested her forehead against his shoulder. "You're right," she whispered. "Oh, Gabriel, she's going to be so horribly hurt."

Gabriel ran his palm down her back. She was so very, very tense. "Hey, you're forgetting that Dixie is the quintessential Southern belle," he said. "Underneath all that taffeta and chiffon is a core of pure and gleaming steel." He kissed the top of her head. "I've got a feeling the lady just might surprise you."

"When doesn't she?" Eve muttered as she straightened and turned back toward the house.

As Gabriel had predicted, Dixie remained unruffled by Eve's halting revelation. "Thank you both for finally letting me know what's going on. While it's very thoughtful of you to be concerned about me, you needn't worry."

"Are you sure?"

Dixie smiled gently. "Positive."

"If you want to talk about it—"

"But there's nothing to talk about, dear."

Eve wondered if her mother had heard a single word she'd said. "Mama, how can you say that? If I were in love with a man, I'd be devastated to discover that not only had he lied to me but he was a convicted felon, as well."

"I can see where that would be quite upsetting," Dixie agreed serenely. "But that's not the case with Harry and me."

Frustration made her words rash. "Mother, you're a fool if you can't see that Harry lied to you. Why, the man is no more a successful businessman than... than... Gabriel." She realized the moment the words had left her mouth that she'd insulted her mother as well as the man sitting across the table from her. Their eyes met, hers filled with chagrin, his amused.

"If Harry was less than completely honest with me, I'm certain he had his reasons," Dixie countered.

"I'm sure he did. Such as the fact that you might not be so willing to marry a common criminal."

"Harry is not a common criminal."

"You're right. Considering how many times he's been arrested, he's an extraordinarily *inept* criminal."

"Eve," Gabriel warned quietly.

"He's not a criminal at all," Dixie insisted.

"I suppose that news flash comes from Madame Leblanc?"

"Now, Eve," Dixie soothed, "you are too young to be so jaded. I love him, darling. And Harry loves me. And I know, deep down in my heart that the arrest report Richard Owens compiled for you is wrong. Just as I know that Gabriel will uncover the truth."

Eve surrendered to the fervent belief in her mother's voice. "Well, I honestly hope you're right, Mama."

"Of course I am." Dixie sounded like her usual cheery self again. She stood up, hugging first Eve, then Gabriel. "Have a successful and safe trip, darlings. Both of you."

"WELL, AT LEAST SHE TOOK the news well," Gabriel remarked as he and Eve drove to her office.

"That's only because she refuses to believe it."

"Perhaps she's right."

"You can't honestly believe Harry is nothing more than a retired businessman who innocently fell into the criminal justice system by mistake, do you?"

Gabriel shrugged. "At this point, I haven't decided what to believe. I think I'll wait until I can talk with the guy face-to-face."

"I can't wait," Eve agreed, thinking that there were several things she wanted to tell Harry Keegan. And none of them was the least bit complimentary.

Gabriel didn't let Eve out of his sight for the remainder of the day, hovering nearby like an overly protective German shepherd. And although she would have been loath to reveal such a thing to him, Eve secretly admitted that his presence was quite reassuring.

IT TOOK GABRIEL less than five minutes to decide that he definitely preferred flying first class. From the wider seats with increased leg room, to the menu he was handed immediately after boarding, to the flight crew hovering nearby, life on this side of the barricade was a vast improvement over the airborne cattle car he was accustomed to. Of course a great deal of this cabin's appeal was because Eve was sitting in the window seat beside him. Overcome with a feeling of happiness, Gabriel took her hand in his.

During the takeoff Eve was a little tense. At Gabriel's questioning glance she said, "I haven't done much flying lately—there's been so much to do in New Orleans. For the past two years I've been assigning more of the travel to Blake Carstairs, my assistant. But there are still times when I need to make the trip myself to make certain things are up to Whitfield standards."

"I can understand that," Gabriel said.

Eve's perfectionism and what he had been viewing as an unfortunate obsession with her work were the precise traits that had put the Whitfield Palace Hotels in a class by themselves. It wasn't that he wanted her to change, Gabriel decided. He merely wanted her to expand her horizons, to see that there was a great deal more to life than work.

The sincerity in his tone was unmistakable, and it occurred to Eve that this was the first time she and Gabriel had discussed her work without getting into an argument. Vaguely understanding that this was a significant milestone, Eve vowed to think about it at the first opportunity. Once they had this case out of the way. Right now, as the jet leveled off at thirty-five thousand feet, she was content to let the light touch of his hand on hers work its soothing magic.

Eve didn't want to destroy the intimacy of the moment, but she finally said, "I have some correspondence to answer."

Once again Gabriel proved impossible to predict. She'd expected an argument, but he released her hand so that he could retrieve her briefcase from the overhead compartment. A moment later he was deeply immersed in the latest Spenser novel he'd purchased at the airport gift shop.

Despite her best intentions, Eve found it extremely difficult to keep her mind on her work with Gabriel seated so close. Every so often their arms or their legs would brush, causing something akin to an electric jolt to pass between them. Gabriel appeared not to notice as he kept his nose in the pages of his paperback novel, seemingly engrossed in the exploits of his fictional counterpart. It was only when the plane began its descent that Eve discovered Gabriel's mind had not been as far away as she'd thought.

Cupping her chin with his fingers, he coaxed her head toward him and covered her lips with his.

The kiss was a symphony of exquisite sensations. His mouth was firm, moist, tasting of passion. The pressure of his fingers, moving tantalizingly up the side of her face, created tingling trails of warmth and need. His skin smelled of soap—crisp and fresh and woodsy, the scent filling her head even as her mind emptied. Her lips turned greedy as desire threatened to rip free.

Gabriel was already half mad for her; if he didn't stop this now, before she took him any further, they'd end up being banned from the airline for life. For a brief, fiery moment, as her tongue touched his, Gabriel thought risking such banishment might be worth it. Then, concluding that maturity and responsibility were not much fun, he reluctantly lifted his head.

"We're on the ground."

Eve's eyes, as she stared uncomprehendingly up at him, were like a storm-tossed sea—wide, dark, swirling with passion. Annoyed at Gabriel for having initiated the fiery kiss, as well as at herself for having escalated it, she fought to regain her composure.

"Really, Gabriel, you had no right to do that," she said as she stuffed the papers she'd been working on into her briefcase.

"How can you say that after everything that happened between us last night?"

"Last night was a mistake," she insisted softly. "One that won't happen again."

"You sound very certain of that."

"I am." The plane had reached the gate, and passengers had begun filing past them. "If we're going to make our flight to Paris, we'd better hurry."

Gabriel remembered the time when he was twelve that a migrating bobolink had been blown off course during a storm and had flown into the kitchen of his family's restaurant. For several long and harrowing hours the bird resisted all attempts to rescue it, flying back and forth between the kitchen and the dining room, beating its wings impotently against the windows. Eventually Gabriel's father had captured the bird in his fishing net, releasing it outdoors to continue its journey.

When he realized that Eve reminded him of that frightened bobolink, Gabriel decided not to push. "Don't worry," he advised with a smile that was no less devastating because it was forced. "We've plenty of time."

They were halfway down the jetway when it occurred to Eve that Gabriel's reassuring words might not have referred to making their connecting flight but to something else a great deal more personal. And more dangerous.

IT WAS MIDMORNING on the following day when they arrived in Paris. Although Gabriel suggested that Eve go to the hotel and get some rest while he met with the local police, he wasn't surprised when she insisted on going with him.

Gabriel had come to the conclusion early in his law-enforcement career that police stations the world over were remarkably alike. In that respect the Paris station differed only slightly in decrepitude from the one in the French Quarter. Paris, too, had been having a heat wave, causing the French detectives to look every bit as miserable as their New Orleans counterparts.

"Here is the information you requested," Inspector Raoul Gauthier said, handing Gabriel a sheet of paper. "All the reported jewel thefts for the last six months."

"There are more than I would have expected."

"As I explained to your unfortunate colleague, thefts have increased considerably this past year."

"Colleague?"

"Detective Murphy. The American detective who was murdered on the way to his hotel." The detective shook his head as he lit a cigarette. "An extremely unfortunate incident."

"Especially for Murphy," Gabriel agreed dryly.

The mention of Michael Murphy cast a distinct pall over the conversation. Given Harry Keegan's extensive record—several of the arrests having involved jewel thefts—it had crossed Gabriel's mind more than once that Dixie's errant fiancé might have had something to do with the detective's death. If that were the case, Gabriel was going to make certain Harry paid for his crime despite his feelings for Eve and her mother.

Something toward the end of the inventory caught his attention. "I see you've captured the men who stole this matching diamond necklace and earrings. Why isn't there any mention of recovering the jewels?"

"Because unfortunately we failed to recover the jewelry."

"They'd already been fenced?"

"No. Stolen."

Eve was incredulous at the idea of so many lawbreakers loose on the city streets. "Someone stole them from the original thieves?"

The inspector lifted his shoulder in a decidedly Gallic shrug. "There is, as they say, no honor among thieves."

"Amazing," Eve murmured.

Gabriel was studying the list more intently. "Do the men in custody have any idea who ripped them off?"

"We believe they do. But they are stubbornly remaining silent, and without their cooperation the crime is, as you Americans say, a dead end."

"Perhaps." Gabriel looked unconvinced. "Well, thanks for taking the time to talk with us," he said, getting up from his chair. "Ms Whitfield and I appreciate your assistance."

"De rien," the inspector responded as he rose to his feet as well. "We law-enforcement officials must stick together, *n'est-ce pas?"*

"Absolument," Gabriel agreed, shaking the detective's outstretched hand.

Gabriel and Eve had left the detective's cramped office and were on their way to the front door of the police station when Inspector Gauthier caught up with them. "There is one additional thing," he said.

"What's that?"

"My men found a card in the apartment where we apprehended the thieves. It read simply *vengeance."*

The single word caused a chill to skim up Eve's spine. Gabriel appeared merely thoughtful. *"Merci,"* he murmured.

EVE WATCHED WITH ADMIRATION as Gabriel deftly maneuvered the rental car through the confusing maze of streets as if he'd been driving in Paris all his life. She had been waiting for him to comment on Inspector Gauthier's information, but so far he'd remained frustratingly silent.

"Well?" she demanded as they pulled up in front of the Paris Whitfield Palace.

"Well, what?"

"What do you think about that card the police found?"

Gabriel had long ago learned to trust his intuition. And right now that sixth sense was telling him that Gauthier had given him the final piece of the puzzle. Now all he had to do was fit all the pieces together.

"I suppose it could be something," he said with a casual shrug as he handed the car keys to the parking attendant. "Then again, it might be nothing. You never know."

"Just what I've always loved," Eve countered dryly as she nodded a greeting to the doorman. "A man with a positive attitude."

As they entered the Paris Whitfield Palace, Gabriel decided that the lobby alone could inspire a year's worth of sermons on conspicuous consumption. Gleaming travertine marble pillars rose at least forty feet above marble floors covered with priceless oriental rugs. A gold domed ceiling boasted Renaissance-style murals; mirrors and oil paintings were massed on the walls. Gold leaf predominated—on the ceiling molding, the wooden balcony, the arms of the brocade Louis XIV furniture and the long, hand-carved registration desk. High above their heads an enormous nineteenth-century French chandelier fashioned from rock crystal, amethyst and pink quartz split the light into dancing, dazzling rainbows.

"Too bad this place wasn't around in the sixteen hundreds," Gabriel murmured.

"Oh?" As they walked toward the front desk, Eve was inspecting the lobby, searching out the single flaw that would make a visit to the Paris Whitfield Palace a less than perfect experience.

Everything about Eve—from her straight spine to her lengthened stride to her acutely critical gaze—reminded Gabriel of his daddy's old hound dog, Jacques, on the trail of an unfortunate opossum. Deciding that Eve would find the comparison uncomplimentary, he didn't bring it up.

"If the Paris Whitfield Palace had been built during Louis XIV's time on the throne," he said, "the guy wouldn't have had to build Versailles."

"Our guests expect the best," she reminded him, running a finger over an ornate crystal table lamp. Not a speck of dust, she noted with satisfaction, making a mental note to write a memo of commendation to the housekeeping staff.

Gabriel couldn't help noticing that everyone—from the liveried doorman to the desk clerk—appeared to stand at attention when Eve approached. All that was missing, he mused, as the bellhop put Eve's bags in one bedroom of the elaborately decorated suite and his in another, was the salute.

"Nice place," he murmured, glancing around the vast living room. A magnum of champagne—French, of course—rested in a bucket he suspected was gold-plated. A silver mesh basket of fresh fruit shared a table with a tray of cheese and biscuits. Gleaming dark caviar was nestled on a bed of ice. "All the comforts of home."

"Believe it or not, some people actually live this way," Eve said as she picked up the telephone receiver. Gabriel suspected the gold and ivory phone was the only reproduction in the room.

"Oh, I believe it, all right."

"You just don't approve."

Having never given the matter a great deal of thought, Gabriel took a minute to answer. "It's not for me to approve or disapprove," he decided. "And although I'll admit such indulgence might be fun occasionally, I think after a while I'd start craving a peanut-butter-and-jelly sandwich."

"The rich are certainly not denied peanut butter and jelly, Gabriel," Eve felt obliged to point out.

She always looked so damn serious when she was defending her father's realm. Actually, now that he thought about it, the only time Eve really discarded that earnest demeanor she wore like a second skin was when they were making love. He wondered idly what his chances were of keeping her in bed for the next fifty or sixty years.

"Ah, but how many of them have you ever known to have really tasted such plebeian fare?" he argued with that devastating grin that she'd given up trying to resist.

"I, for one, can't imagine life without it."

"And you're rich."

"Filthy." Her eyes met his with a calm, level gaze. "Do you have a problem with that?"

"Not at all. Do you?"

Eve couldn't define the sense of relief his answer had caused. She only knew that they seemed to be suddenly discussing something a great deal more serious than food. "No," she said firmly. "I don't."

"Then we don't have any problems."

"I suppose not," she murmured. They exchanged a long, significant look that left her feeling more confused than ever. "I'd better make my call," she said at length.

He could feel her backing away from him again and was damned if he knew what to do about it. *Later*, he promised himself. "Who are you calling?"

"I have a friend, Madeleine Delacroix—actually she's Dixie's friend—who knows nearly everyone in Paris. At least everyone who moves in the circles that attract jewel thieves. If Harry's here, Madeleine will know where to find him. I thought I'd wangle us a dinner invitation before taking a nap."

"Good idea," he said, his mild tone belying the gleam in his dark eyes. "What with jet lag and all, we could both probably use some rest."

"Alone."

"Spoilsport."

"So I've been told," she agreed with reluctant amusement as she dialed the hotel operator.

IT WAS HER INTERNAL CLOCK, nothing more, Eve assured herself as she tossed and turned, trying to get some much-needed sleep before their late-night supper with Madeleine Delacroix. Her family friend had offered the invitation without hesitation, saving Eve the ungracious task of inviting herself.

Despite her hope that Madeleine could provide some information that might lead them to Harry, Eve was less than thrilled with the idea of introducing Gabriel to the stunning society matron. The five-times-married Madeleine Delacroix had never met a man she didn't like, and Eve couldn't deny that Gabriel was a great deal more likable than most. When erotic images of the night she'd spent in Gabriel's bed continued to swirl behind her resolutely closed lids, Eve decided to try reading. With any luck she'd find a book boring enough to put her to sleep.

On the other side of the suite, Gabriel was reminding himself that he was a mature adult, not a horny, sexcrazed teenager. There was no reason that the thought of Eve all alone in that wide canopied bed should have him pacing his spacious quarters like a caged lion. No reason at all. Eve was only a woman, and an argumentative, maddeningly stubborn one at that. She was also too serious for his taste.

"And probably spoiled rotten by her beloved daddy," he muttered, raking his hands through his thick black hair. "Take away the woman's credit cards, and she'd probably go into withdrawal."

When his next thought was of the enticing bits and pieces of satin and lace she could purchase with those pieces of plastic, Gabriel's body began to thud with a slow, persistent ache.

A cold shower would be no help at all, he determined immediately upon entering the mirror-lined bathroom. Unlike most French bathrooms, which offer a tub hardly large enough to bathe a parakeet, this bathtub could hold the entire front line of the New Orleans Saints, with room to spare. A man could swim laps in it. Or make love. Wanting Eve outrageously, Gabriel decided to help himself to more of the food left in their living room. If he couldn't satisfy one hunger, he might as well concentrate on the other.

He found Eve standing in front of the bookcase, clad in a short silk robe the color of cornflowers. The memory of those long smooth legs wrapped around his hips was acutely vivid.

"Looks like I'm not the only one having trouble sleeping," he said.

Despite the fact that her back was toward his door, Eve had known the instant Gabriel entered the room. Taking a deep breath that was meant to calm, but didn't, she slowly turned around. He was wearing the jeans he'd worn on the plane and nothing else. At the sight of all that dark skin, desire flared in her.

"It's undoubtedly jet lag."

"I'm sure that's it." He finally looked away from her scantily clad body to the bowl of fruit. "I've heard a warm bath helps."

"Perhaps." Eve had already found the tub far too inviting for her own good. "I thought I might read."

"Good idea." He selected a shiny red apple from the silver mesh basket and bit into it. The fruit was moist and sweet, reminding him achingly of Eve's mouth. Unable to resist, he moved closer to her. "A massage is reputed to work wonders on jet lag." His gaze moved over her face, lingering on her lips.

Eve swallowed. "Really?"

"Really." He ran a fingertip down the lapel of her robe. The material was smooth and cool to his touch. Gabriel knew that underneath the blue silk her skin would be smooth and warm. "How about it?" His knuckles brushed lightly against her skin, creating a spark.

"You're certainly welcome to give it a try. The hotel has a masseuse on call."

"That wasn't what I had in mind, Evangeline."

He was so close. Too close. "I know."

He slipped a hand inside her robe; her heart pounded furiously beneath his palm. "You want me."

"Yes." Her soft sigh feathered against his lips. Gabriel uncaringly tossed the apple aside as he drew her into his arms. "You don't sound very happy about it."

As he nuzzled her neck with his lips, Eve tried to remember exactly why that was. "I think I'm afraid."

"Of me?" he asked incredulously.

"No. Not exactly."

"Not exactly?" His hands moved to her waist, and a moment later the silk robe drifted to the carpet. Naked, without the trappings of wealth or power, Eve appeared softer. More accessible."

"I'm a different person when I'm with you," she complained softly. "More impulsive. Emotional." Her distressed blue eyes met Gabriel's patient ones. "I don't understand."

"It's called acting naturally, *chérie*," he assured her gently, solemnly. He cupped her cheek in his hand. "Do you know that no other woman has ever made me feel the way you do?" His hand trailed down the side of her face. "No woman has ever made me burn the way you do?"

"Gabriel—"

He shook his head. "I want you to understand how I feel," he insisted. " I want you to believe what I feel for you is special. Unique. Every time I see you, it's like the first time. Every time I touch you, it's like the first time." His words were dark and low, wrapping her in folds of ebony velvet. His fingers skimmed lazily down her torso; they were doing unbelievable things to her nervous system. Beyond words, Eve clung to his shoulders. When his palm pressed against her stomach, she shuddered and leaned closer.

"Tell me you feel the same way," he demanded thickly.

Her body was on fire; flames were licking at her very core. "My God, Gabriel," she gasped as she felt his gently probing touch between her thighs, "can't you tell?"

"I need to hear the words," he insisted, savoring her warm, moist readiness. "I need to know that it's the same for you as it is for me."

Eve's nails sunk into his shoulders as she swayed. "It's the same," she whispered. "It's always been the same."

That was all Gabriel had needed to hear. "Come to bed with me, Eve."

"No." As her hands tore at the frustrating row of buttons, Eve vowed to buy Gabriel a pair of jeans with a zipper at the first opportunity. "Here. Now."

When her fingers curled around his thrusting shaft, Gabriel couldn't wait any longer. "Now." He eased her to the plush carpet.

Outside the luxurious suite, the Paris sun was shining brightly; inside hot winds swirled and thunder roared. With a sexual aggressiveness that would have shocked her at any other time, Eve took Gabriel into the vortex of blinding heat and whirling color with a passion and a fury he could only follow. The air was thick and heavy as he surged into her, and sheathed in her warmth, Gabriel began to move, faster and faster, higher and higher, above the rumbling clouds to where, clinging to one another, they rode out the storm together.

"That sure beats the hell out of a massage," Gabriel said after a long, pleasurable interlude.

"Mmm." Eve pressed her lips against his moist chest, reveling in the warm, musky taste of his skin.

"Provided we're capable of moving, do you want to try to reach your bed? Or mine?"

"Yours. It's closer."

12

THERE WAS, Gabriel decided two hours later, something to be said for waking up beside a beautiful woman. As he carefully brushed back the blond hair covering Eve's face like a curtain, he felt a renewed stir of emotion. Her eyes were closed, her lashes resting on cheeks that blushed with the faint hint of roses underneath her skin. Her full lips were curved in a sensuous half smile that made Gabriel wish he could share her dreams.

No longer the brisk businesswoman, neither was Eve the passionate vixen who'd turned his body to flame. She was, remarkably, the woman he'd fallen completely, unalterably in love with.

The realization that he was in love with Eve was as sudden as it was unexpected. As he glanced at the gilt clock on the marble mantle, Gabriel decided that he'd have to deal with this later. Right now there was business to attend to: the business of finding Harry Keegan before any more bodies popped up to litter the landscape; the business of ensuring Dixie's safety; and most important, the business of keeping Eve close to him long enough for her to realize that as incredible as it might seem, they belonged together.

Pressing a light kiss against her lips, he slipped from the bed. Ten minutes later, after shaving, showering and dressing, he stopped long enough to leave Eve a note. Then, with one last fond backward glance, Gabriel left the suite.

FOUR HOURS LATER Eve was in danger of wearing a path in the ornate design of the antique Tabriz rug. Her first thought upon awakening to find herself alone in the suite was that Gabriel had left her. When a quick check revealed his suitcases still unpacked, she had breathed a deep sigh of relief. It was only then she noticed the note propped against the lamp on a nearby table. It read:

> Out earning my fee. Just in case whoever trashed your condo has followed us here, don't leave this suite without me.

Under any other circumstances his abrupt instructions would have had her seething. Still filled with the pleasure of their recent lovemaking, Eve decided to overlook his arrogance.

By the time she'd bathed and dressed, Eve's patience was hanging by a cobweb-thin strand. What if those men had followed them to Paris? What if they'd taken Gabriel captive? What if at this very minute they had him tied up in some horrible damp place and were beating him, torturing him? Or worse yet . . .

No. Vowing that she wouldn't permit herself to think such thoughts, Eve decided that she could best help by remaining calm. She'd just picked up the receiver to place a call to Inspector Gauthier when she heard the sound of the electronic door key. A moment later Gabriel strolled into the room, looking as if he didn't have a care in the world.

"If you're calling room service, I could sure do with a double cheeseburger," he greeted her with a grin.

Relief that he was safe mingled with anger that he'd had her so worried. "I was calling Inspector Gauthier."

He reached into the compact refrigerator behind the bar, pulled out a bottle of German beer and took a long swallow of the icy dark brew. "Boy, does that hit the spot. That song lyric about Paris sizzling in the summer isn't kidding. It's like an oven out there." He took another drink. "Why were you calling Gauthier?"

"Because I thought something might have happened to you, that's why."

"Worried about me, Evangeline?"

"Of course not." When she wasn't struck down on the spot for her lie, Eve decided not to press her luck. "I was worried sick."

"I left you a note."

"I found it. But when you didn't come right back, I began imagining all sorts of terrible things."

"Oh, sweetheart," Gabriel groaned, putting down the beer to take her into his arms. "You've no idea how good that makes me feel." Desire stirred, but Gabriel ignored it. For the moment. "And although I can't think of anything I'd rather do than go back to bed and try to make up for the worry I caused you, I suppose I should change for dinner."

"That would probably be a good idea," Eve murmured, sounding no more enthusiastic than he.

He tilted his head back and smiled down at her. "I need another shower. Want to come scrub my back?"

"In the interest of arriving at Madeleine's sometime before tomorrow morning, I think I'll pass."

"It's your choice," he said agreeably. "Just don't blame me if word gets out that the management of a Whitfield Palace Hotel was unwilling to oblige a guest."

Winking broadly, he left the room. When she heard the sound of water running in the bathroom, Eve had to restrain herself from stripping off her clothes and taking him up on his enticing but unfortunately ill-timed offer.

EVE COULDN'T REMEMBER ever being so angry. Her irritation had been sparked the moment she and Gabriel had arrived at Madeleine Delacroix's home in Passy. She knew that the area in the 16th arrondissement of Paris was synonymous with elegant living. There was, however, nothing elegant about the older woman's outrageous flirting with Gabriel. By the time they'd reached the main course, Eve had been tempted to dump the tender medallions of lamb right into Madeleine's Dior-clad lap.

"Nice evening," Gabriel said as he drove the rental car out of the cobblestoned driveway. Across the river the Eiffel Tower lit up the night sky.

"Humph."

Gabriel glanced over at her, wondering what it was that had put Eve in such an uncharacteristically rotten mood. She'd been quietly seething all evening long. "The food was great, especially the *Langoustines à la nage aux piments*. I've never had crawfish that way. Madeleine promised to give me the recipe."

"Madeleine's always been a very generous person."

"She's a nice lady," Gabriel agreed conversationally. "I liked her a lot."

"I could tell."

This time there was no mistaking the acid in Eve's tone. "Something wrong?"

"What could be wrong? Other than the fact that a woman old enough to be your mother was practically sitting in your lap the entire night."

Gabriel's lips curved into a satisfied smile. "Could you by any chance be jealous?"

"Of course not," Eve countered, pretending an avid interest in the gleaming gold dome of the Hôtel des Invalides. "I simply think she could have behaved more discreetly."

"Really? I thought she was a model of decorum."

Eve shot him a suspicious look. "You're teasing me again, aren't you?"

"Not at all. If your friend was really coming on to me, Eve, I honestly didn't notice."

His expression, not to mention his tone, was too sincere for her to doubt him. Still, Eve knew she'd not imagined Madeleine's outrageous behavior. "How could you not notice? My God, Gabriel, she couldn't have been more obvious if she'd stripped naked and had herself served to you on one of her antique silver platters."

He put his arm around her stiff, silk-clad shoulders. "As long as you were in the room, I probably wouldn't have noticed that, either."

Her shoulders relaxed, her expression softened and a warm, womanly glow appeared in her blue eyes. "That's a very chivalrous thing to say."

"It's the truth, Evangeline."

His sincerity threatened to be her undoing. Things were becoming too complicated, too fast. Backing away from the intimate moment, Eve turned the conversation to the reason for their late-night supper with Madeleine Delacroix.

"I told you she'd know Harry. Or Farley Thurston-Smythe, as he's currently calling himself."

"So you did," Gabriel agreed. "And it's a lucky break for us that he's going to be a guest at her party this weekend."

"Lucky," Eve murmured. "I notice Madeleine didn't waste any time inviting *you* to the party."

"She invited both of us."

"Right. That's why her hand was on your thigh when she brought it up."

"It was on my knee, and if it makes you feel any better, I was prepared to spill my passion fruit soufflé in her lap if those perfectly manicured fingers climbed any higher."

Eve chuckled, suddenly feeling lighthearted. "I almost did the same thing two courses earlier."

"I'm certainly glad you managed to restrain yourself."

"Oh, really?"

"Really. That would have been a terrible waste of truffles."

They shared a laugh, then Gabriel's expression turned serious. "I spent this afternoon talking with some informants Gauthier was helpful enough to put me on to," he informed her. "The word on the street is that this Avenger guy's been a royal pain in the butt to the underworld for the past three months by ripping off the thieves before they can fence the loot."

"That doesn't sound like a very intelligent career move," Eve mused.

"You wouldn't think so, would you?" Gabriel agreed. "Especially since he's been concentrating on the same gang."

Eve thought about that for a moment. "That, along with that card he left, makes it sound personal."

Gabriel gave her a rewarding smile. "Very good—if you ever tire of the hotel business, I could probably be talked into taking you on as a partner."

There was a hint in his voice that made Eve believe that Gabriel might be talking about something far more serious than a job offer. Deciding that she was jumping to conclusions again, she shook her head.

"Thanks, anyway, but I'm quite happy where I am."

Gabriel shrugged. "Suit yourself."

"Do you think Harry's this Avenger person?"

"Could be. The timing's certainly right. Every Avenger theft has taken place during a period when Dixie said Harry was away from New Orleans."

"So if Harry is the Avenger—"

"We'll be able to nab him at Madeleine's party."

"What if he doesn't show up?"

"Then it's back to the drawing board."

A comfortable silence settled between them as Gabriel drove the car back to the hotel. Eve was the first to break it.

"What are we going to do for the next three days?"

Gabriel had an immediate answer to that, but not wanting Eve to think that all he was interested in was sex, he forced a nonchalant shrug. "There's no point in looking for Harry, since according to Madeleine this Thurston-Smythe character's out of town looking at country estates."

"Do you actually believe that?"

"Not the part about the estates, but I do think he's probably lying low until Saturday night. Let's face it, Eve, if Harry *is* the Avenger, right now he's hotter than TNT. So since there's nothing to do but wait, we may as well schedule a little sight-seeing. Unless you'd rather use the time to run an inspection on the hotel," he offered magnanimously.

Eve reached over and put her hand on his thigh. "I can't think of anything I'd rather do for the next three days than explore Paris with you."

Gabriel covered her hand with his. "I knew from the beginning that you were an intelligent woman. Not to mention being a knockout."

"Ah, yes," Eve murmured, thinking back to their initial meeting. "If I recall, there was something about putting a bag over my head if I wanted a man to concentrate on my mind."

"No fair quoting from my chauvinistic past," he complained. "I've changed."

"In four days?"

"A lot can change in four days," he said mildly.

Knowing his words to be a giant understatement but not wanting to get into exactly how much had changed between them, Eve didn't answer. That didn't stop Gabriel from sensing that once again their minds were on the same track. For now that was enough.

FOR THE NEXT THREE DAYS, to the obvious surprise of the hotel staff, Eve ignored business entirely and opened herself up to all that the famed City of Lights—and Gabriel—had to offer. To her surprise, she found herself having a marvelous time as she allowed herself to bask in all the pleasures Gabriel had brought into her life.

They strolled hand in hand along the tree-lined boulevards, stole kisses in the gardens of the Champs Elysées and laughed at Punch and Judy shows in the Tuileries Gardens. Although Eve had protested when Gabriel asked a sidewalk artist on the Left Bank to immortalize her in a pastel portrait, he proved adamant, and soon she was seated on a wooden stool, trying to ignore the curious gazes and pointed comments of passersby.

Afterward, studying the paper portrait over a bottle of burgundy at a café on the Boulevard Saint-Germain, Eve was stunned to see that the artist had captured all the warmth and love that had been shining on her face as she'd looked at Gabriel.

To Eve's further amazement, she and Gabriel began discovering things they had in common: both enjoyed long walks, Charlie Chaplin movies, jazz and lazy Sunday mornings in bed with the *Times* crossword puzzle. In turn, they shared a distaste for dress-up Sunday brunches, telephone-answering machines (although both admitted ownership of this diabolical invention, claiming it was a business necessity), mandatory office Christmas parties and highway tollbooths.

On other matters, such as the fact that Gabriel's favorite spectator sport was baseball while Eve preferred the ballet, they readily agreed to disagree. It wasn't much, Eve knew—certainly not enough to base a lifetime commitment on—but it was more than she'd ever expected.

It all would have been perfect, had it not been for the gun Gabriel insisted on wearing under his lightweight jacket. But Eve had given up complaining about the weapon and after a while found that she could actually forget its existence for hours at a time.

On the second day of their vacation they spent several hours at the Louvre, working their way through hundreds of saints, kings, archangels, miles of pastoral scenes, and innumerable stiff-spined bourgeois ladies and gentlemen. By the time they got to the enormous gallery housing the Flemish masters, Andy Warhol's soup cans would have seemed like a breath of fresh air.

"Life before Jazzercise," Eve murmured, staring up at a scantily draped trio's ample breasts and roseate derrieres.

"And cholesterol warnings." The freshly killed game, silver urns overflowing with ripe fruit, loaves of dark bread and flagons of wine in the still lifes reminded Gabriel that it had been more than five hours since breakfast.

"The good old days."

Gabriel's attention drifted from the heavy gilt-framed paintings to settle on Eve. She was wearing a full-skirted, white cotton sundress sprigged with yellow rosebuds that he'd insisted on buying her the moment he'd seen it in the window of a Right Bank boutique. Her hair, which she hadn't forced into its customary bun since the night of Madeleine's dinner, flowed down her back like a rippling gold waterfall. Her soft pink lips were unpainted, permitting him to kiss them whenever he got the urge. Which was often. The last time had been nearly ten minutes ago.

"No," he corrected quietly. "*These* are the good old days."

Eve looked up at him, her eyes wide, darkly blue and filled with something he could only hope was love. "You're right," she whispered after they'd exchanged a long, significant look. "These are the best of days."

Smiling, Gabriel bent his head and kissed her because it had been too long.

Unfortunately, the halcyon days passed all too quickly, and it was Saturday. Gabriel had already determined that that night, whatever happened with Harry Keegan, he was going to propose to Eve. He'd have to have been a blind man or a fool not to know that Eve was uncomfortable with intimate discussions. But he'd come to the conclusion, during an afternoon ride they'd taken together along the river on a rented bicycle built for two, that she'd just have to learn to deal with it because he couldn't continue making love to her night after night, day after day, without telling her his feelings.

Tonight, he vowed. After the party.

They were finishing dressing when the gilt telephone rang. Gabriel answered, leaving Eve to listen with building frustration as she was unable to tell anything from his monosyllabic responses.

"That was a friend of mine, Jim Carmichael," he said as he replaced the receiver. "He's an FBI agent living in D.C. The one who ran the check on Harry."

"The check that didn't turn up anything," Eve recalled.

"It didn't turn up anything the first time," Gabriel qualified. "I called him after we arrived here and asked him to run Harry's photo through the system again."

"And?"

"And this time the computer located him."

"Well, I'm certainly not surprised," Eve said as she turned back toward the mirror and slipped her pearl earrings into her earlobes. "After all, with Harry's record it would have been amazing if your friend hadn't found him. I'm surprised it took as long as it did."

"It took that long because Jim was checking Harry's picture against the wrong list."

Eve's curious gaze met Gabriel's in the mirror. "The wrong list?"

"We were looking for Harry in the criminal computer banks, Eve."

"Well, of course you were," she said impatiently, turning around. "That's because Harry's a criminal."

"No. He's not."

Now Eve was thoroughly confused. "He's not?"

"You were right about him not being a businessman, but he's not a criminal, either."

"Then what is he?"

"He's a career FBI agent."

"Harry's an FBI agent?" Eve could have been no more surprised if Gabriel had told her that her mother's fiancé was a Soviet spy.

"Retired," Gabriel clarified. "But I think he decided to solve one last case before hanging up his gun for good."

"A jewel theft?"

"No. A murder."

"The murder of the agent in his apartment?"

"Uh-uh. The murder of Michael Murphy."

"Isn't that the name of the detective Inspector Gauthier mentioned the other day? The one who was killed?"

"That's right. He was killed right before Harry arrived in New Orleans," Gabriel said. "Harry Keegan is an alias, Eve. The guy's real name is Patrick Xavier Murphy. Michael Murphy was his son."

"Oh, my God," Eve breathed. "So Harry is the Avenger after all."

"I'd say that's a pretty accurate assumption. He obviously created a false identity for himself, then began causing trouble to draw the man who ordered his son killed out into the open."

"Do you think he could be planning to meet that man tonight?" Eve asked incredulously. "At Madeleine's party?"

"It's a distinct possibility."

Eve's expression, as she looked up at him, was filled with open admiration. "Richard Owens was right," she said. "You are the very best detective in New Orleans."

"Speaking of Richard Owens," Gabriel said casually, "one of his men has been following us since we left New York."

Eve drew in a quick breath. "You're kidding!"

"I never kid about things like that, Eve."

"But I never saw him."

"That's because you're not the expert detective."

"But why?"

"I have a feeling we'll find out tonight."

Something occurred to Eve. Something decidedly unpleasant. "Gabriel, if that man follows us to the party, if he's involved in the jewel thefts—"

"He isn't going to be following us anywhere," Gabriel assured her.

Eve studied the almost smug look on his face. "Gabriel, you didn't..." The possibility was too horrendous to consider. A moment later Eve realized she'd overreacted. "You wouldn't have hurt him," she decided. "Not unless it was in self-defense."

She trusted him. And believed in him. As far as Gabriel was concerned, such faith showed her love for him more than her enthusiastic lovemaking ever could.

"I'm glad you have such faith in me," he said.

Her eyes smiled up at him. "Of course I do. What did you do with him, Gabriel?"

"He's on his way to the laundry."

"The laundry?"

"Bound and gagged and wrapped up in the sheets from the ninth floor," he confirmed. "I figure by the time he gets free and reports to whoever is paying him, we'll have cleared up the Case of the Disappearing Fiancé."

He hooked his arm around her waist, pulling her to him for a quick, hard kiss. One thing he really liked about Eve—she never complained about a guy smearing her lipstick or mussing her hair like so many other beautiful women he'd known.

"Come on, sweetheart," he said, "let's get the business part of the evening over with."

Eve's smile, as she looked up at him, was intimate, impish. "So we can get down to the pleasure."

Gabriel laughed. "I knew you were a fast learner."

As they left the spacious hotel suite, a small, rebellious part of Eve almost hoped Harry wouldn't show up. Because once they'd found her mother's lover, once they'd settled things once and for all, she and Gabriel would be forced to return to New Orleans and their own lives, and this idyllic, magical time would come to an end.

"I've had a good time," she said as they took the elevator down to the street floor. The walls of the elevator were lined with smoked-glass mirrors; Gabriel couldn't help noticing that her sorrowful reflection was in direct contrast to her words.

"Me, too," he agreed, putting a friendly arm around her waist. "We'll have to do it again sometime."

Hope was a hummingbird, fluttering its delicate wings inside her heart. Eve steadfastly ignored it, as she had been doing ever since the first night she and Gabriel had made love.

"The next time I have to hire a detective to track down one of my mother's errant loves, you'll be my first choice." Her feigned cheeriness was belied by the moisture gleaming in her eyes.

"Eve—"

His serious look was too intense for comfort. Before he could continue, the elevator suddenly stopped, and a well-dressed middle-aged couple entered, letting Eve know exactly how a punch drunk fighter must feel at the welcome sound of the bell. Leaning back against the glass wall, she breathed a sigh of relief as she waited for her heartbeat to return to normal.

IT WAS LIKE SOMETHING from a fairy tale. Tall willowy trees framed the doorways of Madeleine Delacroix's palatial country estate; tiny white lights had been strung through the branches and around nearby stone pillars. Guests—women dressed in long, beaded gowns and men earnest and elegant in black tie—drifted from room to room, glasses in hand. In the main gallery the deep-toned claret and forest-green silk moiré table-cloths echoed the colors of the trompe l'oeil woodland scenes on the far wall.

"I think I've died and gone to heaven," Gabriel murmured as he eyed the buffet tables where glittering ice sculptures held shrimp, lobster, Scotch smoked salmon and gleaming caviar with *Crème fraiche*. A trio of tuxedoed waiters continually replenished the sterling Buccellati serving trays.

"We're here to find Harry Keegan," Eve reminded him.

"First rule of surveillance," Gabriel countered as he plucked a grilled oyster from its bed of coarse pink sea salt and placed it on a plate, "is to blend into your surroundings. Besides, it's probably a mortal sin to let food like this go to waste." He analyzed a piece of puff pastry. "What do you suppose is in this?"

Eve took a sample taste. "Salmon. With a touch of dill."

"Terrific." Two more pastries joined the oyster on his gold-rimmed plate.

"I'll say this for you," Eve said, watching as he made a tiny yellow plum tomato adorned with pearls of salmon roe disappear. "You certainly don't let your work spoil your appetite." Her own stomach felt as if a pair of giant condors had taken up residence.

Gabriel rolled his eyes in appreciation as he sampled a slice of the heart-shaped roasted squab surrounded by buttered leeks and gleaming black truffles. "I didn't get any dinner."

"And I suppose that was my fault?"

"Of course it was."

"Funny, that's not the way I remember it."

Gabriel stopped filling his plate long enough to give her a slow, intimate appraisal. She was wearing her hair up tonight in what he supposed was meant to be a sophisticated style but only served to draw a man's attention to the fragrant nape of her neck. Her Grecian-style white crepe gown was elegant, giving her the unapproachable air of a goddess. Gabriel decided that he rather liked the way she could slip into that cool persona—especially when it served to keep other less enterprising men at a distance.

His eyes, as they roamed her face, were warm with remembered passion. "It was your fault for looking like a midnight fantasy come to life," he murmured. "And for smelling like someone who'd just stepped out of the enchanted forest. Not to mention feeling like—"

"Gabriel, there he is," Eve hissed, grabbing Gabriel's arm as she spotted the familiar figure across the vast room.

Gabriel followed her gaze to the tall, iron-haired man in formal dress who was edging toward the doorway. "Damn," he muttered, "the guy's timing leaves a lot to be desired." He put his plate down with a fond parting glance. "If I'm not back in twenty minutes, call Gauthier."

Eve grabbed his arm. "Wait just a minute."

"We're wasting time here, Eve," Gabriel countered in a low, warning tone.

"I'm coming with you."

"The hell you are."

"But—"

His expression could have been carved from granite. "I'm not taking any chances, Eve. Not with you."

She could hear the steel in his voice and decided that discretion was in order. "Promise that you'll be careful?"

He bent his head, pressing a quick, hard kiss against her frowning lips. "I'll be back before you know it."

As Eve watched him walk away, it crossed her mind that she'd never seen a man who looked as striking in black tie as Gabriel Bouvier. Remembering the gun Gabriel was wearing under his jacket, Eve waited a few cautious seconds before following him from the room.

The party had spilled out into the garden, and sounds of laughter and conversation floated on the soft, perfumed air. As Gabriel made his way through the thick green maze of hedges, he heard a faint sound behind him. He stopped, head cocked as he listened intently. Then, drawing his revolver, he slipped around the corner. And waited.

Eve had no sooner turned the corner of the leafy hedge when she was jerked into the bushes. Before she could scream, a large, dark hand covered her mouth.

"Dammit, I thought I told you to stay put." Perspiration soaked Gabriel's starched white shirt as he realized how close he'd come to harming her. "You could have been killed, woman!"

"You never would have hurt me," Eve said as soon as he'd released her. "I know you, Gabriel. You're much too controlled to go shooting at every stray sound."

"You sound very sure of that."

"I'm sure of you," she countered calmly, turning her attention to the greenhouse a mere twenty yards away.

The slanted glass walls glowed with a warm yellow light. "Is Harry in there?"

"Yes." His face in the silvered moonlight was grim.

"Then the meeting's going off as planned."

"Seems to be."

The case had bothered him from the beginning; there were too many contradictions, too many coincidences. When he saw the second man enter the greenhouse, the final piece to the puzzle that was Harry Keegan had fallen into place.

"And the head of the jewel-theft ring is in there with him?"

"They're both in there—Harry, or Murphy, or whatever you want to call him. And Richard Owens."

"Are you saying that Owens found Harry before we did?"

"No. I'm saying that Owens used us to find Harry for him." When the sound of a gunshot suddenly pierced the night air, Gabriel gripped Eve's shoulders with a bit more force than necessary. "Don't you dare move so much as an inch from this spot." A moment later he was gone.

Dying to go with him, but not wanting to endanger his life by distracting him, Eve reluctantly complied with his grim order. She watched and waited, her heart in her throat, as he crept toward the door of the greenhouse, revolver in hand.

There was the sound of glass breaking as he kicked in the door. Then a silence that seemed to go on forever. Finally, unable to stand the suspense any longer, Eve raced toward the greenhouse, terrified of what she might find when she got there.

What she found was Gabriel, standing just inside the doorway, his revolver pointed at Harry Keegan, aka Patrick Murphy, who in turn was holding an ashen-faced Richard Owens at gunpoint. An angry red stain was darkening Murphy's sleeve.

"What the hell are you doing here?" Gabriel asked, glaring down at her.

"I was worried about you."

"I'm fine. It's these guys we need to worry about." Gabriel turned his attention back to the man who was inadvertently responsible for bringing Eve into his life. "Don't do it, Murphy. He isn't worth it."

Murphy's eyes were like flint in a rough-hewn granite face. "The bastard killed my son."

"I had nothing to do with that," Owens protested. "Some of my people overreacted."

"Your people?" Eve asked. "What people? What are you talking about?"

"I don't give a damn who pulled the trigger," Murphy growled. "You're the one who gave the order. You're the one who's going to die." His face was set and implacable as he glanced over at Eve and Gabriel. "Why don't you two just go back to the party and forget you saw or heard any of this."

"You know it's too late for that, Murphy," Gabriel said in a low, calm voice. "If you want to keep this quiet, you're going to have to kill Eve and me, as well. And I don't think you're willing to do that."

"I don't give a damn about keeping it quiet. All I want is revenge for Michael's death. After that the cops can do whatever they want with me."

"I'll be sure to tell Dixie you said that," Eve retorted.

Her relief at finding out Harry wasn't a criminal was overshadowed by the thought of having to return to New Orleans and explain to her mother that the man she loved was in prison for murder.

"She loves you," Eve said softly.

"And I love her."

"You love my mother?"

"Of course I do."

Eve looked long and hard into his steely gray eyes and believed him. "Yet you disappeared without saying a word."

"I wanted to keep her safe." He turned to Gabriel. "Surely you can understand that."

"Perfectly," Gabriel answered grimly, shooting Eve a significant look. "So why don't you think of Dixie for a change and give up this revenge scheme? As it is, with all the grandstanding you've been doing you're lucky not to have been killed. Like your partner."

"Partner?" Murphy looked back and forth between Gabriel and Owens. "What in the hell are you talking about?"

"Peterson was found dead in your apartment. Apparently one of Owens's contract men mistook him for you."

Murphy's eyes glittered dangerously as he turned his attention to Richard Owens. "Dave Peterson and I were partners for fourteen years," he said flatly. "We were like brothers. He had a wife and three kids. And his first grandchild is on the way."

"He's the only one who knew what you were doing, isn't he?" Gabriel guessed. "He used the agency computer to create your phony rap sheet and kept you up-to-date on the information the Bureau was getting from Interpol."

"Not to mention compiling a lot of the information that led me to Owens." Murphy rubbed his face with a weary hand. "I've loved four people in my life," he murmured. "My first wife, who died when Mike was eight, my son, Dave Peterson and Dixie. And this son of a bitch killed two of them." The click as he cocked the gun was deafening in the sudden silence.

"Look," Owens blustered, putting up both hands in front of him, "we can still work this out. Just let me go and you can keep all the jewels you've stolen—no one need ever know. You'll be a rich man. Richer than you ever imagined."

Eve had never seen anything as frightening as the intensity on Patrick Murphy's face. Fury burned in his eyes, and his mouth was set in a harsh, grim line. When he suddenly turned toward Gabriel, his weapon still in his hand, she thought she felt her heart stop.

"You're right," Murphy said woodenly, extending the gun butt first toward Gabriel. "He isn't worth it."

Eve squeezed her eyes shut for a long, thankful moment. When she opened them, Gabriel was busily tying Richard Owens's hands behind his back with a length of green garden twine.

"You've been shot," she said, turning to the man she'd known as Harry Keegan.

He shrugged massive shoulders clad in an ill-fitting dinner jacket. "It's just a scratch. I never expected Owens to be willing to do his own dirty work—guess I made a mistake."

"I guess you did," Eve murmured as she rolled up his shirtsleeve to examine the injury. Although she was certainly no expert on gunshot wounds, it looked as though the bullet had merely grazed the skin.

"I think you'll live," she diagnosed. "But you'll probably have to get a new jacket for the wedding—this one's had it."

The older man's eyes softened as he looked down at her. "I thought you were dead set against your mama marrying me."

"I was in the beginning," Eve agreed as she exchanged a faint, intimate smile with Gabriel. "But a lot can change in a week."

13

"I CAN'T BELIEVE IT."

Hours later, as the rising sun tinted the Paris sky a soft, delicate pink, Eve was still trying to accept the events of last night. After a lengthy conversation with Inspector Gauthier, she and Gabriel had returned to their suite at the Paris Whitfield Palace. Patrick Murphy, having had his flesh wound treated at a nearby hospital, was now ensconced in the Ambassador suite on the floor below, and the jewelry he'd stolen had been returned to the authorities.

Richard Owens was in jail. He'd been visited by a local attorney, as well as the American ambassador, and was now awaiting extradition to the United States, where, along with his other crimes, he would stand trial for the murder of Maxwell Harkins, aka Mad Max.

"It's been a weird eight hours," Gabriel agreed. Under normal conditions he'd feel satisfaction after solving a case, especially one as complex as this. But he knew that he wouldn't be able to relax until he and Eve wrapped up one last detail. The little matter of their future.

"I still can't believe Richard Owens is capable of killing anyone," Eve murmured, rubbing her temples where a headache was threatening.

"Greed is a powerful motivator," Gabriel said mildly.

Eve sighed. "I suppose so. Imagine him using his security firm as a cover for an international theft ring."

She sighed. "He never would have known about Harry if I hadn't gone to him in the first place. That makes me responsible for that poor FBI agent's death."

"You can't look at it that way, Eve. You were only trying to protect Dixie. Peterson and Murphy were professionals, and they knew the risks."

"I wish I could believe that."

"You should, because it's true. I'd never lie to you, *chérie*."

His look was so solemn, so caring, that a lump rose in her throat. Eve was almost grateful when the ringing phone shattered the silence.

"That'll be the overseas operator," she said unenthusiastically.

"Want me to break the news to Dixie?"

"That's very nice of you, Gabriel," Eve said as she reached for the telephone. "But Dixie's my responsibility."

Personally, Gabriel thought it was past time Eve learned that it wasn't necessary to carry the entire world on her shoulders. From what he had seen so far, Dixie was perfectly capable of taking care of herself. And even if she hadn't been Patrick Murphy was standing by in the wings, more than willing to take on the job of keeping Eve's mother out of trouble.

Knowing this was no time for another argument on work versus pleasure, he kept silent as Eve explained the events of the past eight hours. After ten minutes Eve turned to Gabriel. "She wants to speak to you."

"Well," Eve said, when he hung up the receiver a minute later, "that certainly didn't take long."

"She wanted to thank me for finding Harry. Patrick," he corrected.

"I take it he's already been in touch with her."

"He called her as soon as he arrived here at the hotel. Oh, by the way, Dixie asked what I thought about a double wedding in the garden." He waited for Eve to say something, anything. When she didn't respond, Gabriel took a deep breath and dove into the dangerous conversational waters. "I said it sounded great."

Eve's mouth had gone as dry as dust at the same time that her arms and legs had turned to stone. As Gabriel approached, she couldn't have moved if she'd wanted to.

"Why don't you stop fighting it?" he murmured as he drew her into his arms. "I love you, Evangeline."

"Gabriel—"

"And you love me." He cupped her jaw and lifted her distressed gaze to his.

"Sometimes I think I do, but—"

"You love me," he repeated, his voice weighted with emotion. "And in my book, when two people love each other, it's time to get married."

"I can't," she whispered softly.

Her soft words were not that much of a surprise. The pain surging through his veins was. Gabriel had thought he'd been prepared for her rejection. He'd thought he was willing to be patient, to wait for her to see that what they had together was special. Unique. Obviously he'd thought wrong.

"Why not?" he asked quietly.

"We haven't known each other long enough to even be discussing anything as permanent as marriage."

She made marriage sound more like a business merger than a commitment two individuals in love made to spend their lives together. "I hadn't realized there was a timetable for falling in love." Only Gabriel knew the herculean effort it took to keep his voice low, his tone mild. "What does a guy have to do? Make an appointment with your secretary?"

"Gabriel, please, you're being unreasonable."

"Unreasonable," he muttered under his breath. Nothing about Eve had been easy; why had he expected this to be any different? Taking a deep breath, he decided to try again. "Let's see if I've got this straight. I'm in love with a woman who, although she's afraid to admit it, is in love with me. Since I want to spend the rest of my life with this woman, I've asked her to marry me. I find that eminently reasonable."

"It's too soon," Eve repeated. "We both have our own lives, our own work."

"I'm not asking you to give up your career, Evangeline."

"I know. But I'm not even certain it's possible to combine marriage and a career successfully. Five years ago the magazines were filled with articles telling women they could have it all. These days that brave talk is beginning to look like just one more fairy tale handed out to gullible women foolish enough to buy it."

It took every ounce of Gabriel's self-control not to push. He'd thought during their time together that Eve had opened up, learned to be more spontaneous in her personal life. Obviously he'd miscalculated badly.

"All right, how about we start out with something simple?" he suggested with what he hoped was an unthreatening, coaxing smile. "Move in with me."

"Oh, Gabriel." Eve sighed, running her hands through her hair.

"Still too much of a commitment?" he inquired easily. Inside, his heart, which he'd never given to any other woman, was being ripped to shreds. Gabriel had never known love could hurt like this. He'd never known he could hurt like this.

"How about getting pinned?"

Nothing.

"Going steady?"

Still nothing.

Gabriel thought he saw moisture glittering in her eyes, but he wasn't sure. "Stop me when I hit on something you can handle."

Eve felt the sting of rebellious tears and resolutely blinked them away. "You don't have to be so sarcastic. Honestly, Gabriel, you make common sense and forethought sound like flaws."

"And you make love sound like something to be negotiated by a team of high-priced attorneys. Why in the hell can't you stop analyzing this to death and follow your instincts?"

Follow your instincts. He made it sound so easy. It probably was for him. And for Dixie. Eve, on the other hand, needed facts. Guarantees.

"Don't you understand?" she complained with something perilously close to a sob. "This has all happened so fast; I need time to think."

Gabriel's control, which had been hanging by a thread, was in danger of snapping, and he knew if he didn't get out of here soon, he'd say or do something that he'd regret for the rest of his life. "All right, you win. You've got your time, Eve."

With a painful, muffled oath he drew her to him, wanting to feel her body against his one last time. She felt so warm, so soft, so right. As his hands spanned her hips, drawing her into the cradle of his thighs, Gabriel could feel her slowly responding, beginning to relax. God, how he wanted her! In his life. And right at the moment in his bed, where he could set about convincing her that what they had together was capable of surviving a lifetime.

Releasing her quickly, before he was tempted to do something he'd detest himself for later, Gabriel forced himself to walk away. He stopped in the doorway just long enough to look back at her standing in the center of the ornate suite. She looked so small. So alone.

"Think fast," he advised with a smile that was a pale ghost of the one she'd come to love.

Unable to answer past the lump in her throat, Eve could only nod. Then he was gone, leaving Eve to stare after him for a heartbreakingly long time. And then she wept.

GABRIEL BOUVIER WAS HOT.

It was August, the temperature was in the nineties and the level of humidity was inching toward a record high, even for New Orleans. The French doors to his cramped second-story office were open, but the air outside was torrid and heavy, providing no relief as he watched a baseball game on the portable television that was perched on the corner of his cluttered antique desk.

It was the bottom of the seventh, and the Mets's Jesse Orosco was on his way to shutting out the Braves at home once again. Gabriel figured he knew exactly how frustrated the Braves were feeling. His shirt was sticking to his back, and he was fantasizing about closing up shop for the day and going out for a tall, cold beer when she walked in the door, looking fresh and cool in a sleeveless white silk dress, sheer white stockings, high-heeled white pumps and a wide-brimmed white straw hat with a navy-and-white-striped band. Beneath the hat her hair was coiled into a neat bun at the back of her neck.

"There wasn't anyone in the waiting room," she said to explain entering his office without being announced.

Gabriel turned off the television. "My secretary, Fayrene, only works half a day on Wednesday, and my new partner is down at Sears getting fitted for a tux."

"For his wedding."

"That's right."

"It's this Saturday, isn't it?" Eve asked, knowing full well the date of her mother and Patrick Murphy's nuptials. Other than her continual fretting over Eve's ill-fated romance, Dixie had been talking of little else for the past two-and-a-half weeks.

Gabriel leaned back in his chair, put his elbows on its scarred wooden arms and studied her over linked fingers. Overhead the lazy paddle fan beat ineffectively at the clammy air, reminding him that he'd hoped to get out of the office early. "That's right."

"I suppose you'll be attending."

"Wouldn't miss it for the world. After all, I am partially responsible for uniting the happy couple." Silence settled over them. "Why don't you have a seat?" Gabriel suggested finally, gesturing toward the chair on the visitors' side of the desk.

Eve glanced around the office. The black-and-white tiles covering the floor were still scuffed, and the metal file cabinets and bookshelves lined up along the institutional gray walls were still piled high with dog-eared manila folders, lined yellow pads, newspapers, law books and telephone directories from what appeared to be every parish in the state. It was a depressing thought to realize that the world hadn't come to an end just because her own life had been turned upside down.

For what had to be the millionth time since she'd made the decision to come here today, Eve felt her courage waning. It had been ten days since she'd received the check she'd made out to Gabriel Bouvier Investigations back in the mail. That it had been torn into confetti-size pieces hadn't been an encouraging sign, but still she had waited, hoping that given enough time, Gabriel would realize that a lengthy courtship was both sensible and practical.

But after more than two long and unbelievably lonely weeks had passed, Eve had come to the conclusion that sensible and practical were not all they were cut out to be. More than a little desperate, she decided that it was high time to put her heart before her pride.

Ignoring the patched vinyl chair, Eve brushed aside some papers and perched on the corner of Gabriel's desk. Twisting her fingers together, she looked up at him through mascara-darkened lashes with a look that Scarlett O'Hara would have envied. The scent of imported bath soap mingled with a mysterious mélange of woodsy oakmoss and dark musk.

"I've a terrible, terrible confession to make."

The heady elixir of fragrances surrounding her filled his head, creating an ache deep in his loins. "That line sounds vaguely familiar."

"It's from *The Maltese Falcon*." When she crossed her legs, Gabriel was treated to a glimpse of lacy white garters that only served to increase his discomfort.

"You've read it."

"Several times. I seem to have become obsessed with private detectives lately." Leaning forward, she ran a pink-tinted fingernail slowly up his thigh. "I don't have to tell you how utterly at a disadvantage you have me," she said silkily, quoting the Dashiell Hammett novel.

His blood simmered under her tantalizing touch; her scent was like a mist over his mind. "I have trouble envisioning you at a disadvantage."

"Oh, but I am." A surreptitious glance at his lap revealed that his body was not as immune to her as he would have liked. Encouraged, Eve licked her lips with a patently seductive gesture she had borrowed from last night's late, late movie. It had worked wonders for Marilyn Monroe; perhaps it might work for her, as well. "I'd have never placed myself in this position if I didn't trust you completely."

"That's another quote," he managed, stifling a groan as Eve's fingers brushed over the most vulnerable part of his anatomy.

"That's right." Eve touched a finger to her smiling lips, then pressed that same damp fingertip against his mouth. "Brigid O'Shaughnessy says it just a few pages after she's offered Sam Spade her body in payment of his fee. You've a very good memory, Gabriel. And you're clever. Just like Spade. The moment I walked into this office, I told myself that finally, here was a man smart enough, courageous enough, to help me."

"Is that right?" he asked unbelievingly.

She nodded, her gaze solemn. "I wanted you from the first."

"Well, you sure weren't alone in that."

"What I hadn't wanted to admit, not to you or Dixie or most of all to myself, was that I began falling in love with you that day."

Gabriel went suddenly still. "What are you doing here, Eve?"

Eve slid off the desk, deliberately closing the French doors before settling herself in his lap. Encouraged when he didn't dump her off onto the scuffed linoleum floor, she began unbuttoning his shirt. "I think that's quite obvious, Gabriel," she murmured silkily. "I've come to seduce you."

"If you're thinking of paying off your fee like Brigid O'Shaughnessy, you can forget it. This isn't necessary."

Eve's smile was positively beatific. "Poor Gabriel, you are so horribly tense. You really need to learn how to relax and experience pleasure, don't you, darling?" Her lips skimmed across his flesh, reveling in the rich male flavor she'd been afraid she'd never know again.

"Evangeline—"

"I do so love the taste of your skin, Gabriel," she murmured, gathering in a gleaming bead of moisture with the tip of her tongue. "It tastes dark. And warm. And forbidden. Like sex."

Her words, the touch of her hand, her lips as they wreaked havoc on his body caused desire to spread, hot and insistent. Pins scattered over the black-and-white floor as he thrust his hands into her hair. "You've changed your scent."

"Madame Leblanc blended it especially for me."

"Madame Leblanc?"

"It's a love potion," she revealed with a low, husky laugh.

The idea of his beloved, practical Eve actually shelling out good money for one of Madame Leblanc's voodoo concoctions was as incredible as it was wonderful. "You're kidding."

"Not at all." She pressed her lips against the wild, out-of-control pulse at the base of his throat. "I picked it up this morning—is it working?" she asked innocently.

His answering laugh was harsh and ragged. "You know damn well it is," he complained as her agile fingers went to work on his jeans. The sound of his zipper—she was glad he'd switched from buttoned jeans—was audible. "Evangeline, *ma belle*, as badly as I want to make love to you, this is my office." The tightening in his body escalated to painful proportions. "Someone could come in."

"Don't worry—I put out the Closed sign and locked the door behind me."

"I didn't see you do that."

Her eyes danced with a wicked feminine laughter. "I have very clever hands," she murmured, proving her claim by caressing the growing length of him.

"You are a very dangerous woman, Evangeline Lorraine Whitfield."

"I am?"

"Don't play the innocent with me, lady. I'm the one you shared that bubble bath with in Paris, remember? Not to mention the night we made love so many times I practically needed a wheelchair to make it downstairs to breakfast the next morning."

Eve tossed her head. "We had breakfast in bed. And if you felt that I was taking advantage of your body, Gabriel, you should have complained at the time instead of waiting until now."

"I'm not complaining—I'm merely pointing out that underneath those severe little business suits you wear like a suit of armor lurks the heart of a wanton, lascivious witch."

"I know." A look of wonder crossed her face. "Do you know that I hardly ever used to think about sex? And now it's just about all I *can* think about. Day in and day out. And the nights are even worse.... Why, you'd never believe how much I fantasize about making love to you after the sun goes down. I'll be lying in my cold, lonely bed, and all I can think about is the way your skin gleams bronze in the moonlight, how your clever, wicked lips can make my body flame and how exquisitely right it feels when you're inside me, moving in and out and in and out...."

"My God, Eve!"

"It's actually become an obsession," she said, ignoring his ragged interjection. "Why do you suppose that is?"

"Perhaps it has something to do with love."

"Perhaps it does," Eve agreed softly.

Two and a half long weeks of celibacy were taking their toll, and Eve's intimate touch was quickly bringing him to the brink. Not wanting to be the only one suffering this erotic torture, Gabriel's hand delved under her white skirt, skimming up her silk-clad thighs to discover secret delights.

"Didn't your mama ever tell you that proper Southern ladies don't leave the house without their underwear?"

"My mama also told me that a Southern lady uses all her womanly wiles when she's out to catch herself a husband," Eve countered.

"And is that what you're out to do?" His finger dipped into a moist, intimate crevice, causing a thrill of desire to shimmy down her spine.

"Yes." Eve's eyes, filled with passion and love, bore not a hint of hesitation. "I want to be your wife, Gabriel. And mother to your three children."

"Three?"

She nodded. "Two boys and a girl."

Two sons. And a daughter who looked like Eve. It was almost too much to hope for. "Madame Leblanc again, I presume."

"Dixie had her throw our stones last night," Eve confirmed. "And while I still don't really believe in her, I can't deny that the idea of making babies with you is frightfully appealing."

She framed his face with her hands, her expression more earnest, more appealing than he'd ever seen it. "I love you so much, Gabriel Bouvier, that I swear I'll literally wither up and die if you don't marry me."

His slow smile gave her his answer first. "If that's the alternative, I don't see that I've got much of a choice," he drawled in that deep, velvety voice Eve knew would still thrill her when she was ninety. "Damn," Gabriel said suddenly. "You've got me so crazy that I almost forgot." Reaching into the top desk drawer, he took out an envelope and handed it to her.

"Airline tickets?"

"What would you say to honeymooning on Bora Bora?"

Joy, pure and golden, bubbled up in her heart as he put his hands on her hips and lowered her body unerringly over him. She couldn't remember ever feeling so light, so free. Why, if Gabriel wasn't holding her so tightly, she'd probably float right out the window and disappear over the gulf.

"Mr. Bouvier," Eve said laughingly as she pressed her lips against his smiling mouth, "I do like your style."

Harlequin Superromance

Here are the longer, more involving stories you have been waiting for... Superromance.

Modern, believable novels of love, full of the complex joys and heartaches of real people.

Intriguing conflicts based on today's constantly changing life-styles.

Four new titles every month.
Available wherever paperbacks are sold.

Step into a world of pulsing adventure, gripping emotion and lush sensuality with these evocative love stories penned by today's best-selling authors in the highest romantic tradition. Pursuing their passionate dreams against a backdrop of the past's most colorful and dramatic moments, our vibrant heroines and dashing heroes will make history come alive for you.

Watch for two new Harlequin Historicals each month, available wherever Harlequin books are sold. History was never so much fun—you won't want to miss a single moment!

ATTRACTIVE, SPACE SAVING BOOK RACK

Display your most prized novels on this handsome and sturdy book rack. The hand-rubbed walnut finish will blend into your library decor with quiet elegance, providing a practical organizer for your favorite hard-or soft-covered books.

Only $9.95

Approximately 16" x 8" when assembled

Assembles in seconds!

To order, rush your name, address and zip code, along with a check or money order for $10.70* ($9.95 plus 75¢ postage and handling) payable to *Harlequin Reader Service*:

Harlequin Reader Service
Book Rack Offer
901 Fuhrmann Blvd.
P.O. Box 1396
Buffalo, NY 14269-1396

Offer not available in Canada.

BKR-1A

*New York and Iowa residents add appropriate sales tax.